ON A SUMMER NIGHT

Gabriel D. Vidrine

A NineStar Press Publication

Published by NineStar Press
P.O. Box 91792,
Albuquerque, New Mexico, 87199 USA.
www.ninestarpress.com

On a Summer Night

Printed in the USA
SunFire Press Imprint
First Edition
April, 2018

Print ISBN: 978-1-948608-40-4

Also available in eBook, ISBN: 978-1-948608-36-7

Fourteen-year-old Casey is determined to have fun this summer going to camp with his best friend, Ella. His overprotective mother frets that attending this one instead of trans camp like he's always done will cause problems, but Casey has his heart set on going stealth anyway.

His mom just might be right.

All Ella wants is love for her best friend, and she's determined to set him up with someone, despite Casey's protests that he just wants to have fun, not get involved in a summer romance. But things get complicated when camp bully Ryan focuses his energies on the two friends. At least Casey's cute bunkmate, Gavin, appears interested in getting to know him better, making Casey rethink the whole romance thing.

Until he finds out Gavin and Ryan are good friends.

Summer camp turns into so much more when Casey has to decide if Gavin is worth pursuing, friend of a bully or not.

There's just one more problem: Ryan knows Casey is transgender.

For the boy I was, the book I could not find.

Chapter One

"DO YOU HAVE your socks?" my mother called up the stairs.

"Yes, mother!" I shouted back down at her. Of course I had socks. But I double-checked the large footlocker anyway, scrabbling through it until I found them. They were buried under my binders, but there they were.

"Don't forget towels!" came another shout up the stairs.

She knew me well. I always forgot something. I went back to my bathroom and rummaged around in the linen closet until I found enough towels for the trip.

When I got back to my room, Mom was staring down into my trunk, her hands on her hips. "Anything else?" she asked, eyeing how much was in it.

"I hope not."

I tossed the towels in the trunk, only to be crushed into a hug from her. "I'm going to miss you Casey," she said into my hair.

I patted her awkwardly. She meant well, but ever since I announced my desire to transition two years ago when I turned twelve, she'd gotten super overprotective and clingy. "I'll miss you too, Mom." I did mean it, but it was going to be a relief to be away from her for almost two weeks. Even though I'd never been away from my parents that long before, not even at trans camp.

She squeezed me harder until I gasped and then let me go. "Are you sure you want to do this?"

"For the millionth time, yes," I said, rolling my eyes.

"Okay. I'll get your dad to get this down the stairs," she said, and then she was gone in a whirl of brown hair and scarves.

I shook my head at her back and pulled out my phone to text my best friend, Ella. *Almost ready. U?*

I knew she wouldn't answer right away (she actually hated her phone, the weirdo), so I nervously went through my list again to make sure I hadn't forgotten anything. I needed a distraction.

While I was rummaging, my dad, a big guy who had prematurely gone bald so he always wore an ugly hat, had lumbered up the stairs and was frowning down at my trunk. "Are you sure you need all that?" His voice was very deep.

"Yeah, Dad." My phone buzzed in my pocket, but I ignored it. "It's almost two weeks."

"Twelve days," he said.

"Yeah, I know." I scratched at my head, slightly embarrassed to talk about my transition stuff with my dad. "I, you know, need some extra stuff." I thought of the binders lying next to my socks.

He glanced at me and nodded, and then looked quickly away. He hadn't been as supportive of my transition as my mom. When I first told him, he blurted, "But you're a girl."

We stood there in awkward silence for a moment as I wondered what I should say to him, father to son. But he hadn't yet called me his son.

He cleared his throat, still not looking at me, and then crouched and heaved up the trunk onto a roller cart he'd carried up the stairs. It was going to be a pain getting it down on the cart, but at least he wouldn't kill his back picking it up this way.

I helped him maneuver it down the stairs, wishing not for the first time I could start hormones. I wanted to be as strong as my dad, but I wasn't old enough yet. Well, I was, but my parents wouldn't approve it until I was sixteen. I figured Dad was the one holding out, because Mom would give me whatever I wanted.

Two more years.

When we finally got the trunk down the stairs, I pulled my phone out. Ella had texted back.

Ella: *Yeah, loading the car. Are you ready?*

Me: *Yes! Just gotta say bye.*

Ella: *We'll be there soon.*

"Ella and her parents are going to be here soon," I told my parents.

Mom had argued long and hard about how I was getting to camp. She wanted to take me, but I wanted to go with Ella and her parents. My friend and her brother had been going to this camp for years, and her parents knew exactly how to get there. Mom pursed her lips and crossed her arms over her chest. "Okay. Are you sure you have it all?"

Annoyance flared up. "Yes!" I said.

"Don't take that tone with your mother," Dad warned.

I closed my mouth and let the anger subside. It wouldn't do to get into an argument with them now. They'd probably not let me go, whether or not they had already paid for my spot. And summer camp wasn't cheap; I'd seen prices on the website.

"Sorry," I mumbled, and Mom pulled me into another hug.

"Be safe, okay?" she said. "I wish you wanted to go to the trans camp instead."

"Mom, please!"

"Okay, okay, I know. You want to go to regular camp like any regular boy."

"I went to trans camp last year," I said.

"I know, and you loved it. That's why I wish you'd go again."

"Stop worrying so much, Mom," I told her. "The kids won't hurt me."

She didn't look convinced when she finally let me go. It was true; trans camp had been fantastic. But everyone there knew I was trans. I wanted to go someplace where I didn't always feel trans. I knew it was impossible, but I wanted a shot at it. All the other kids at trans camp had loved it, because they'd said they could shed their trans identity there. Since everyone was trans, we got to talk about other things. It made it less special, which was, in reality, a relief.

And that was the problem for me. I just wanted to be like any other boy. And all the other boys went to summer camp like the one I was going to, not to trans camp. I wanted to be a boy with the other boys.

"Are you sure? Kids can be crummy to each other sometimes."

"Yeah, I know, Mom. Switched schools because of it, remember?" I rolled my eyes.

My dad walked out of the room then, and Mom watched him leave with pain in her eyes. He went into their bedroom—the big master suite on the main floor of the house—and closed the door. I looked away, too, not wanting to see the expression on her face.

I pulled out my phone and went to sit on the couch to wait for Ella.

Me: *Please come soon. My parents are being parents again.*

I sent it as a snap, which I knew Ella didn't really like. In it, I looked bored as I lounged on the sofa.

Ella: *haha we're on our way.*

Me: *Good bc this is killing me.*
Ella: *What was it this time?*
I told her. We'd been friends for absolutely forever, as long as I could remember. She was the first person to know I was trans, even before I did. She'd never once misgendered me after I came out, and never used my birth name, though she'd known it all her life.

By the time we finished texting back and forth about it, she wrote one final one:
Ella: *pulling up!*
"They're here!" I called out.

Mom had wandered off to restlessly putter, but she shouted from upstairs that she was coming. I didn't know where my dad was, but right then, I didn't care. I wouldn't have to deal with his disappointment in me for almost two whole weeks.

The doorbell rang, and I ran to answer it. When I opened the door, Ella threw herself at me and squeezed me in a big hug. She was all legs and long blonde hair, classically beautiful. Normally, she wore a lot of makeup, but her face was scrubbed clean, though her yellow hair was in perfect waves. She grinned at me, showing her braces (which she hated). The rubber bands were pink.

"Ready?" she asked.

My dad came out of the bedroom then, and Mom also reappeared.

They helped load the footlocker into Ella's parents' van and then stood around talking with them for too long. Mom was interrogating her father about the route. Ella and I piled into the back, alone. They would also be picking up her brother from camp to bring him home, but until then, it was just the two of us.

Over the whole summer, the camps up in Ankley Springs held sessions for groups of kids of different ages. Her brother, Brian, was too young to be in the same one as Ella, which was a relief because he was an annoying scab. Only thirteen- and fourteen-year-olds would be in our session. Luckily for Ella's parents, Brian's session ended right as ours was beginning.

"So," Ella said, "are you ready for romance?"

"Come on," I said, blushing. "We're not even there yet."

"There's going to be lots of cute guys," she said, raising an eyebrow. "And it's queer as hell."

"Shh." I glanced furtively at my parents. I'd been out to them as trans for years now, but they didn't know I was bisexual. One thing at a time. I think my parents avoided the subject of dating for fear of finding out too much, or having to field weird questions from other parents. Dating boys as a girl was fine, but dating boys as a trans boy might send them over the edge. Mom tried so hard to think of me as a boy, and this might short-circuit her. I didn't want to know what my dad would say or do.

"Sorry." Ella mouthed it at me, ducking her head. "I forgot."

"It's okay. They'll have to learn eventually." I just wasn't sure now was the best time. Maybe when I was eighteen.

My parents finally released Ella's from interrogation, gave me one more hug, and then watched as we pulled out of the driveway. I waved at them as we took off down the road.

We'd be heading way out into rural Virginia, almost to the border of West Virginia, up in the mountains. It was a long drive, but Ella's parents were prepared.

We watched cartoons on their DVD player and ate salty snacks all the way there, so it wasn't too bad of a trip.

After a couple of hours, Ella's mother, Mrs. Brenson, finally chirped out, "We're here!"

I looked up as we passed a rustic wooden sign that proclaimed Ankley Springs, and pulled onto a dirt track from the paved road. Trees loomed around us, spreading their leafy branches until it seemed we were driving through a green tunnel. I loved the trees, and I smiled as we passed from sparse forest into true woodlands. We also started climbing, the van jouncing and rocking over the rutted road. Ella, who sometimes got a little carsick, turned a little paler and went quiet.

Nervousness and excitement warred in my chest. Going to camp as a trans boy was going to be fraught with problems. I was going to be staying with boys, changing with boys, constantly around boys. They would notice my binder. But I had plans in place, and the adults, the counselors, all knew. Even if the kids found out I was trans, it shouldn't be a problem.

I hoped.

Ahead of us, the forest opened up into a tiny little town. All of the buildings were white with green roofs and trim. It was relatively flat and open right here, but we were clearly still in the mountains. The tree-covered hillsides loomed around us, dotted with houses propped up on stilts. The road was still dirt, but it was in better shape here. We passed a small pool off to one side, and I looked at it longingly.

We finally pulled up into a huge field full of cars and people and, after being flagged to a parking spot, we all got out. The field was easily larger than the size of a regular football field, with an enormous pavilion at one end. Trees surrounded the entire thing. All the other people were heading toward the pavilion, crowding around a few tables set up on the concrete where adults in bright blue shirts were checking names off of lists.

Ella and I ran to the pavilion ahead of her parents. Our trunks would be driven up to the campsite later, so we wouldn't have to worry about them yet.

Brian, tall for his age and gangly with white-blond hair, was there, milling about waiting for us. Ella went straight to him and nearly pushed him over. "Hey!" he shouted, and they got into a half-hearted wrestling match.

I wandered around the pavilion instead of watching them fight. There were two basketball hoops, but they had been cranked up out of the way. I noticed Christmas lights had also been strung up in the rafters, and my heart skipped a beat. There was a dance on the last night of the session, and it would take place here. I couldn't help but think how romantic it might be to dance under the twinkling lights...

I shoved that thought away. I wasn't sure yet how queer I could be here, despite what Ella had said. People might get weirded out over me being trans as well as me being bisexual. Romance was not what I wanted out of this trip, but the thought was still a pleasant one...

Mostly.

I wandered back to Ella and Brian who, by the sullen look on both their faces, had been yelled at by their parents for fighting. We got in line and waited briefly. Though we were there for only a few minutes, it felt like an eternity. I was impatient to go and have fun.

I got signed in first, and the perky girl who checked off my name—Casey Stearns—gave me a name badge, a T-shirt, a water bottle with the logo of the camp on it, and my cabin assignment. I was in cabin four. "You might also want to turn off your phone," she told me as I edged aside so Ella could check in.

That was the only bad thing about going camping. I pulled out my phone, and sure enough, even though I could get service just about anywhere else, I had nothing out here.

I told myself it was for the best and switched the phone off. Leaving it on would run the battery down while it searched for service. I'd come to camp to relax and have fun, and having my phone meant my parents could reach me. Knowing my mom, if she could, she'd call me every hour desperate to know if anyone had been mean to me since we'd last talked.

Ella was in cabin eight, and she explained to me that all the boys' cabins were the furthest away, in cabins two through six. The girls' cabins were seven through eleven.

"What about cabin one?" I asked.

"That one isn't used in this session," she said. "There's also cabin twelve, but some of the extra counselors stay there."

"What's cabin one used for?"

She shrugged. "I think for other camping programs. I've never seen anyone in there before."

As we waited for Brian to get checked out, Ella explained, "This camp is actually used by a number of programs. This one gets it during the early summer, and another one gets it during late summer. There's even a fall one, but that's for homeschooled students and nontraditional students who have the time to come up for a couple of weeks during the school year. I think there's even a religious camp, because there are shrines all over the place."

"Interesting," I said, not all that interested as I scanned the other campers, looking for anyone who might also be in cabin four. I wanted to know who I was going to be living with for the next two weeks, and if they were going to be exciting or not.

Brian finally got checked out, and we went back to the van. We climbed in once more and drove up the mountain to the actual campsite. The road was rocky and bumpy and very steep, but we made it up with no problem.

The cabins, sitting on their stilts, were strung out along one side of the road and pushed up against the rising ground. We were almost at the top of the mountain, but not quite, and the road continued past the cabins on upward. The cabins were painted a dark brown, nearly lost among the dirt and tree trunks, except for large yellow plaques with the numbers painted on them. Two larger buildings on the opposite side of the road were also painted the same dark brown. Signs above the doors proclaimed them to be the Washington Lodge and the Lincoln Lodge.

Ella's parents helped me unload my trunk from their van and get it up the short flight of stairs to the cabin.

I didn't go in, but instead, nervously hugged Ella. "See you soon, okay?" It would be great if we got to hang out at some point. I suddenly didn't want to be alone without my best friend or my parents to protect me. For one sick moment, I thought of riding back down the mountain with Brian and Ella's parents and going home. But it passed as she squeezed me back.

"You'll be fine," she said. "Just be yourself."

We shared a smile, and she got back into the van to be driven to her own cabin. We locked eyes through the window, and she held my gaze until she was too far away, her bright hair the last thing I could see.

The door of the cabin opened up again, and a tall man with a riot of dark hair leaned out. He had light brown skin and dark eyes, and a goatee. "Hey there!" he called. "You must be Casey!"

"Yeah," I said.

He strode down the stairs and stuck his hand out. I shook it, and it was warm and dry. "I'm the counselor for the coolest cabin—cabin four! My name's Wade."

"Hi, Wade."

He waved me into the cabin. There were already a couple boys inside, and they looked up to stare at me as I came in. I tried to look confident and cool. I was a boy, just like them. But I self-consciously ran a hand through my short hair, reassuring myself that it was, indeed, quite short.

At school, I didn't have to worry so much about how I carried myself or whether I "passed" as a boy or not. Everyone there knew I was trans. But here, no one knew. I was trying to be stealthy about it, in hopes I could live my life like any other boy. It meant I was going to have to examine everything I did and said to make sure it didn't seem girly or weird. It was exhausting, but I needed to see if I could do it.

"Hi, guys," I said, and my voice didn't shake. *Go me.*

The cabin was tiny, with five bunk beds crammed in head-to-end around the room. Four of those beds were already occupied. There was also a tiny set of shelves containing a clock and a miniature stereo—one with a music file player plugged into it, but it could also take antiquated CDs—and a vase with a bunch of wild flowers soaking in water.

Wade said, "Pick a bunk wherever you like."

I debated whether I wanted an upper bunk or a lower bunk. I was scared of falling out of an upper bunk, but I didn't like the idea of someone being above me. All the other boys had picked upper bunks so far. Wade's bed—the only one that was clearly claimed but didn't have someone sitting on it—was a lower one, but he had strung up a curtain so it was mostly obscured. That would have been ideal for me, but I hadn't thought of it. Upper bunk it was.

My trunk was in the middle of the floor, so I shoved it under the bed I'd chosen and then hopped up onto the top bunk.

"Great!" Wade said, grinning around at everyone. "We'll do introductions once everyone gets here, okay? For now, just settle in!"

The other boys looked at each other and at me, and it was all uncomfortable silence. No one had phones to stare at to occupy the time. I hopped back off the bunk, slid out my trunk, and got out my sheets. I'd rather do something useful than sit around worrying about how I looked.

I puttered, making my bed and rearranging the stuff in my trunk, just to have something to do. When I couldn't do anymore without looking strange, I pulled out a book from my trunk, replaced it under the bed, and then hopped back up.

None of the other boys had made their beds yet and were just staring around at each other suspiciously. A few other boys came in, and Wade had them pick a bunk.

A cute redheaded boy picked the one underneath me, and I tried unsuccessfully not to blush at him. He was short, but that wasn't a problem for me since I was pretty short, too. At least he was still taller than me. I was also a sucker for freckles, and he had a lot of them.

Over the next hour, I tried to distract myself by reading as the rest of the cabin filled up. As it got louder outside the boys in the room seemed to relax. They began to talk and laugh with one another.

Once every bunk was filled, Wade interrupted my reading.

"Hey guys, welcome to cabin four!" His enthusiasm was catching, and I couldn't help but smile at him. His grin was wide, his eyes twinkling. "Are you ready to be the most awesome cabin this summer?"

There were some half-hearted agreements. His face fell, and he tilted his head. "Come on, guys, let's get excited about camp! This is going to be a great summer! I'm used to cabin four being the best cabin all summer, and you're not going to break my streak are you?"

There was some laughter, and he relaxed into a smile again. "Okay, let's try again. Are you ready to be the most awesome cabin this summer?"

We all cheered this time. It was silly, but I couldn't help but join in. I wanted this to be an awesome cabin, too.

"Better! Now, here's the rules. Every morning, we clean the cabin. Everyone pitches in, okay? I'll have a signup sheet for chores, and we rotate them. One person a day will get out of chores."

That sounded pretty sweet.

"Cabin inspections are during breakfast, so we'll find out at lunch who won the Clean Cabin Award, okay?"

"What do we get as an award?" one boy asked.

"Glad you asked!" Wade said. "We get in line for dinner first, and we get to be first in line for Canteen. You'll want that. There's no soda here, except at Canteen. You get first choice, and we always run out of something."

"Sounds lame," another boy said.

"Hey, hey, none of that here," Wade admonished, pointing a long finger at the boy. "That's not a cabin four attitude, okay? We have to pitch in and work together if we want to have fun." He cleared his throat and went on. "No one goes down the mountain without a counselor. We'll line up for meals as a cabin and go down as a whole unit. We have a buddy system with the girls' cabins, and we're buddies with cabin nine."

My stomach sank. Ella was in cabin eight, so we wouldn't be buddies.

Wade continued, "But don't worry too much about that. You can sit with whoever you want at meals."

That was a relief.

"Lights-out is at ten, and there are no exceptions. Except—" and he waggled his eyebrows at us "—for those cabins who manage to get the Clean Cabin Award more than five times."

"That's a lot," the redheaded boy said.

"Yes, it is, but it's possible. Next week, if we've managed to rack up the award every day, then we can stay up and have a pizza party one night. And we get to have lights-out at eleven for the rest of the session."

"That's more like it," said the boy who had complained about the award being lame.

"Thought you'd like that," Wade said, shaking his head.

"Anyone caught slacking or breaking rules will either be forced to clean the cabin or one of the lodges all by themselves, or be sent home, depending on the severity. So don't break any rules."

He set down the rest of those rules then, which were mainly things like don't litter, don't talk back, be on time to lights-out, no fighting...

"Now," he said, once he was finished. "Let's introduce ourselves. Tell us your name. And..." He scrunched up his face like he was thinking really hard. "...what is your favorite board game?"

He pointed to the boy on the top bunk nearest him. He was tiny, with sandy-blond hair, and eyes and lips that were too big for his face. "Hey, I'm Mike, and I've never played a board game." He looked like he meant it, and that we were stupid for having played them.

"That's too bad, Mike," said Wade, not rising to the bait. "Do you play video games? What's your favorite?"

Mike sighed and said, "I like *World of Orcs* and *Bloodcraft*."

"Great games!" Wade said, and I wondered where he got all that optimism and enthusiasm. He must have it injected into his system somehow.

The next kid, a tall black boy with dark brown skin, a shaved head, and a quiet voice, was Alex who liked Monopoly. Next, it was me, so I said, "Hey, I'm Casey, and I like *Pioneers of Noran*." The red-haired boy below me was Gavin who also liked *Pioneers of Noran*. Inwardly, I cheered. Outwardly, I leaned down casually and gave him a thumbs-up. He grinned back. Things were definitely looking up.

We continued around the room. There was a Nick who had dark hair and eyes, a Geoff ("with a G") with brown hair and blue eyes, a Tanner who had a brown rattail and looked like he belonged at a tractor pull, an Elliot who was tall and dark and was already showing the beginnings of a mustache, a shy brunet named Tyler, and finally Ryan, a defiant blond with dark eyes who refused to give a game he liked.

"Okay then," Wade said, glossing over Ryan's rudeness. Ryan narrowed his eyes and clenched his jaw but didn't talk back. "I told you before, but I'm Wade, and I like all board games. If you're bored and need something to do, just come find me, and I'll play whatever you like!"

He continued, clearly changing the subject. "We have a while before dinner, so relax, go explore, whatever you want. Just be back in the cabin by four thirty. We need to get everyone together to line up for dinner, and we leave at five."

I hopped off of the bunk and smiled at Gavin. "Hey, what did you think of the new expansion pack?" I asked him, hoping our interest in Noran would strike up a friendship.

"I loved it!" he said, and we were off.

I ended up sitting on his bed, while we jabbered on about the game. After we had exhausted what we could think of about it, we moved on to ourselves. I told him where I was from and was disappointed to learn he didn't even live in the same state. "Yeah," he said, "we came here from West Virginia."

That was too bad. Well, at least he was going to be good company for the next couple weeks.

After that, our conversation trailed off, and he excused himself. He had friends to go meet. I figured I might as well explore and see if Ella was free yet.

I left the cabin and strolled down the road toward the two lodges. There was already a crowd of kids there, lounging on the low stone wall in front of the Lincoln Lodge, and going in and out of both buildings.

I picked a lodge and went into Washington. It was a huge open space, with wooden benches pushed up against the walls. Most of the benches were already occupied with kids chatting with one another. I was ignored. I made the loop around the lodge and then exited, trying not to feel embarrassed and out of place. A lot of the kids appeared to know each other already, and I figured they'd been coming to camp since they were small, like Ella.

Lincoln Lodge was different, partitioned into a few rooms with a screened-in porch in the back. Picnic tables had been set up in each room, and one room even had a fireplace and rug. A set of shelves next to the fireplace contained a few ancient-looking books covered in dust. On one of the tables were some pieces of paper. I casually walked over and peered over the shoulders of some of the other kids.

"What's this?" I asked one.

She glanced at me, smiled, and said, "Morning activities! Sign up for what you want to do tomorrow morning after breakfast."

"Do we have to do any of them?" Wade hadn't said anything about activities.

"Sort of. You're supposed to sign up, but as long as you're around camp, you should be fine. But some of them have limited slots, so sign up as soon as you can if you want to do them."

"Thanks."

She beamed at me, and I felt my face flush. She was cute, too, with brown hair cut into a bob and bright blue eyes.

Girls didn't flirt with me very often. I wondered if this was how it felt. Or was she just being nice? I didn't want to be the jerk that mistook one for the other.

Once enough people were out of the way, I scanned the options. There was something called Greek dodgeball, a football game, swimming, how to make friendship bracelets, and how to use a compass. All of them except for Greek Dodgeball and football had limits. There was even one that had only five slots, and it was entitled "Super Secret But Amazing Activity." No one had signed up for it yet, and I wasn't sure I wanted to, either.

Swimming was a no-go. I couldn't swim in my binder and didn't want to explain why I wore it, and I wasn't about to get into a full bathing suit. It was the one thing I missed about not presenting as a girl anymore. I'd been a decent swimmer and enjoyed the water. But now it was too fraught with difficulties. I wasn't a fan of football. The compass one might be interesting, but I wanted a chance to talk with Ella first before we signed up for radically different things.

I wasn't a fan of dodgeball either, but I had never heard of Greek dodgeball. What was the difference? I didn't particularly relish the idea of being hit with plastic balls, but I didn't see much choice if Ella didn't want to do the compass one.

After dithering for a few minutes, I ended up signing up for the compass activity instead anyway. I almost wrote down Ella's name, too, but I didn't want to get her mad at me. The friendship bracelets thing sounded a little silly, but if she'd rather do that, I could switch my name over. There were enough slots it shouldn't be a huge problem.

After that, I had to answer nature's call, so I wandered down to the bathrooms.

Even though I'd been going into the boys' restroom at school for a year now, my heart still skipped a beat any time I approached one I hadn't been in before. I ignored the feeling, as I always did, and entered it more confidently than I really felt.

No one was in there, so I picked a stall at the far end and did my business.

As I was finishing, the door banged open and a herd of boys came in, their shoes making a racket on the concrete floor. I froze instinctively, my heart suddenly in my throat. They were laughing and chattering and acting like normal boys. I relaxed and was about to step out when I heard one boy say, "Hey, guys, I heard there's a girl in with the boys."

I bit my lip.

Another voice, "What the fuck does that mean?"

"It means," said another voice, "that we have some queer living in one of the cabins."

"Anyone know which one?"

"Nah. Everyone's being really tight-lipped about it."

"That's against my religion."

There was mean laughter. I closed my eyes and tried not to care. They didn't know who it was who was trans, only that there was someone at camp who was. Someone had blabbed. I knew the camp director had only wanted the counselors to know. The fewer who knew, the better, for just this reason. Someone always talked.

I was going to have to brace myself for the inevitable. I would be outed at some point before the end of camp, and this proved it. If people were already suspicious, it wouldn't be too long before I'd cease to pass, and I'd have to start thinking now about how I wanted to handle it. It was frustrating and a little frightening this had come out so soon. And it wasn't even the first whole day.

I could start telling people myself and hope for the best, or wait for it to come out, possibly at a bad time or in a bad way. Neither option was great. There were always more options, but the longer I waited, the fewer there would be.

There was nothing for it: I was going to have to talk to Wade about it. I'd hoped we could have waited awhile longer for this conversation, but it was clear now we couldn't.

The boys finished their business, and once they were gone, I crept out of the stall and washed my hands. The water was bitterly cold, and I shivered. It wasn't just from the water.

I trudged back up the hill to the cabin, but was glad when I heard my name shouted.

Ella was running toward me, and she threw her arms around me in one of her crushing hugs. "Everything okay?" she asked when she saw my face.

I looked around. There were a lot of people nearby. "Yeah, tell you in a minute. First, did you sign up for anything?"

"Yeah! Dodgeball!"

I was so astonished I didn't know what to say at first.

"Hey, no, it's not like regular dodgeball," she said when she realized why I wasn't saying anything. Then she reconsidered. "Well, it is, but it's more fun than that. You should come, too!" She flashed pink braces at me.

"I signed up for the compass thing." I wasn't sure I wanted to put myself in the path of someone with a big ball and a hatred for trans people.

Ella's face fell a little, but then she grinned again. "Don't worry; there's plenty of time for dodgeball! The compass thing sounds fun. I'll see if there's still slots."

We went back to the lodge, and Ella was able to switch her name to the compass activity sheet. I was relieved. She pulled me outside and down the road toward the empty cabin number one. "We're not supposed to go all the way there," she explained, "but we can get a little privacy near it."

Once we were out of earshot, I told her about the encounter in the bathroom.

"Oh, I'm so sorry Casey. That's terrible. Did you see who it was?"

"No, unfortunately. I didn't want to leave the stall."

I didn't want them to notice me, when they were already primed to look for people who didn't seem to belong. I hadn't thought to peek out to see who they were. Part of me didn't want to know. What if Gavin had been one of them? What if any of the boys in my cabin had been one of them? Chances were good, but I couldn't know for sure.

She squeezed my arm in sympathy and then checked her watch, and her mouth made a big round O of surprise. "Come on, we're going to be late for dinner."

We ran back down the road, hand in hand. A few people tittered as they saw us together, but we were used to that. We split up and went to our respective cabins.

Wade eyed me and then the clock. "Cutting it close, Casey!"

"Sorry."

Everyone else was there. I scanned the faces, wishing I could read the thoughts behind them. Had any of them gone to the bathroom recently? Did any of them suspect? Alex was the only one who noticed me looking, and he met my gaze coolly. I looked away, embarrassed at getting caught.

"Okay!" Wade said. "It's time to go!"

We trooped out of the cabin and onto the road. Already, a large crowd had gathered, and everyone was talking animatedly, excited about finally being at camp and away from our parents. We lined up according to cabins and buddies. The order would rotate, so cabin two and cabin seven went down the mountain first, followed by everyone else. The next day, cabin three and cabin eight would go down first, and so on. Only the cabin that won the Clean Cabin Award would break that system, as they would get to go first.

Our two cabins intermingled, and I got to see the buddies we had in cabin nine. There were ten girls, just like there were ten of us boys in cabin four. They ignored us, giggling in cliques already. I wasn't up for breaking into one of those groups yet. I didn't care that it might look weird for a boy to hang out with the girls—a lot of my friends back home were girls and boys—but since it might be considered weird, I was going to stay away. I didn't need to have anyone wondering about me because I happened to like hanging out with girls. There were a couple of pretty girls in the group, but no one was as cute as Gavin.

So I tried to hover as near him as I could without looking creepy. He was deep in conversation about something with Geoff and Ryan, so I couldn't strike up one about Noran again. I'd be walking alone.

Once everyone was lined up—there were a lot of us, and the noise we made was pretty incredible—the signal was given to head down. We walked down the mountain, being admonished to stay in our groups until we got to the dining hall. It was a long and difficult walk, and I was surprised. The trip up had been so short in the car, but it was going to be a chore doing it at least three times a day for meals. The road was uneven and rutted, and I tripped over large rocks a few times. It was steep, too.

I tried to stay near Gavin, but two of the other boys from our cabin had joined in the discussion. I was too shy to cut in, and I had no idea what they were talking about. Instead, I noticed Alex walking alone but near me. He either didn't notice me looking in his direction or didn't want to acknowledge it.

Oh well. At least I'd get to sit with Ella once we were there.

We made it to the meadow with the pavilion but passed it up and kept going down the mountain. On the right, we passed the pool again, which I threw another longing look at. Someday, I'd be able to swim and not have to worry about my body at all. I'd just swim like any other boy. But that was a long time off in the future.

A wave of depression passed over me.

It was lonely being trans sometimes. You wanted to get close to people but also feared it. You wanted to be "normal" and like everyone else, but there was no way you could be. Not for the first time, I wished I wasn't trans. I wished I had just been born with the right parts.

Some of my trans friends didn't like the "born in the wrong body" narrative ("Bodies can't be wrong" was what my friend Annie always said), but it still fit some of us. My body had never been right. And when I started puberty, it came up with a whole host of new problems. My breasts had already started to grow, and it had terrified me. I didn't want them. I cried and screamed when Mom took me to buy my first bra when I turned ten. She hadn't understood it, and neither had I. It had felt like giving up, though, like I'd lost something valuable I couldn't identify. I'd been so confused I refused to wear the bras at first, and only relented when it was too uncomfortable not to.

Luckily, I got put on puberty blockers as quickly as possible after I came out to my parents. But it hadn't stopped me from getting small breasts. That was why I wore the binder and would need surgery later in life. I tried not to dwell on it too much, but reminders like the pool didn't help. I looked away.

After the pool came more civilization. We passed large white houses with green trim, where old men were out watering the lawn and children were playing tag. No one had phones, which weirded me out a little. I wondered vaguely if we could get service this far down the mountain. Surely we could? There were people here, and they needed phones, didn't they?

The crowd veered off toward one of the large houses, and we made our way to one of the outbuildings off to the side. A counselor, who wore a name tag that said Trisha, Cabin Seven, stood on the stairs, blocking everyone from going inside. A screen door blurred the view inside, but I could see people moving around, placing jugs of water on tables.

Trisha waited until everyone was lined up again and then led her cabin into the dining hall.

It took a while for me to get there, but Ella had saved me a spot. I slid in between her and another girl, an Asian girl with short-cropped dark hair and somewhat pale skin. She smiled shyly at me, and I gave her one back.

Ella said, "This is Lily," and pointed at the other girl.

"Hi, Lily. I'm Casey."

"You're in cabin four?" she asked.

"Yep."

"My brother's in there."

"Oh right—Nick."

"Yeah."

I hadn't gotten to know Nick yet, so we lapsed into silence after that. I felt awkward, but Ella, as usual, smoothed everything over.

"The food here is great," she told us both. "All-you-can-eat rolls, and the fried chicken is good! They don't serve it all the time, though." She looked around, as though searching for the missing fried chicken.

"You've been here a lot?" asked Lily.

"Yep! Every year since I was eight!"

"Wow," Lily said, and I agreed.

I relaxed a bit after that and was able to enjoy the meal. The food was tasty, though simple. We started with a salad, and then we had barbeque sandwiches. This wasn't canned or premade barbeque, either. It tasted like it had been smoked right outside, tender and juicy.

"They bake the bread here," Ella explained, handing me another roll. It looked like it had been baked in a muffin tin, with two large lobes boiling out over the top. "We call these butt buns." She giggled. I snorted and Lily tittered.

I slathered more butter than I should have on my roll. It really was good. We also had corn on the cob, boiled potatoes with sour cream, sweet tea, and pink lemonade—that everyone called bug juice for some reason.

By the end, I was stuffed. But we had dessert, too, which was a variety of cookies, mounded on plates. I took two but would have taken more if I hadn't already been so full.

After dinner, we were allowed to socialize, so the crowd mixed up a bit more. Lily got up to go talk to her brother, and Ella and I were left mostly alone.

"So?" she asked, her expression eager.

"Ella, come on."

"No, no, tell me, who do you like?"

Part of me hated that Ella was ace and aro—asexual and aromantic—and that she lived what fantasies she did have vicariously through me. She was on the ace spectrum, which meant specifically for her that she wasn't really interested in dating, sex, or romantic relationships. I sullenly wished she would go and get herself a boyfriend to get off of my back. But that was a mean thing to think about my friend, so I never said it out loud. I didn't particularly like that I had those thoughts about her.

I sighed dramatically and tilted my head in Gavin's general direction. He was surrounded by friends, including Ryan, all of them chattering as though they'd known each other for a long time.

"Name?" she asked.

"You don't know him?"

She shook her head. "Haven't seen him before."

So he was a first-timer like me, but he seemed to be doing a lot better for himself than I was. "Gavin," I whispered, fearing he would hear me.

"Oh, nice name. He's cute, I guess. Anyone else?"

"Not really."

"Come on, Casey! Look around!"

I did, scanning faces now that I could see everyone gathered in one spot. There were some cute people, but I wasn't sure I found any of them attractive enough to pursue. No one stood out. Except Gavin.

I hadn't come to date. I kept telling myself—and Ella—that, but neither of us appeared to be listening.

Well, my eye was caught by one of the counselors I hadn't seen before. I blushed suddenly then, and Ella noticed. She grabbed my arm and shook me. "Who, who?" she hissed in my ear.

I nodded in his direction and she tsked at me. "Going after one of the counselors, shame on you, Casey. That's Lars, anyway." She flicked her hand in dismissal.

Lars was a gorgeous man. Not handsome, not attractive, but gorgeous. His face was feminine, almost suspiciously so, and his hair was long and candy-floss in texture. It was the palest white I'd ever seen on a person. His skin was ruddy in spots but so pale I wondered if he had albinism. His eyes were clearly dark, though, big and brown. Weirdly, he was wearing a sweater in this heat, and it was an obnoxious shade of pink.

"What's with him?" I asked.

"He's a little weird. Quiet, but nice. He plays guitar."

"Of course he does. What cabin is he in?"

"He's one of the out-of-cabin counselors. He doesn't have his own; he stays with the others in town. You should know better, though, Casey."

I did. He was pretty, but he was definitely way too old.

"Are you sure no one else our own age?" Ella lamented.

"Yeah, I'm sure."

"Okay, so what are you going to do about Gavin?" She mouthed his name, huddling in close, her shoulders hunched for maximum plotting.

"I don't know. Probably nothing. Look, Ella, this really isn't the place for romance, okay? Not now." I wanted a chance to be a kid, and not always a trans kid. Romance complicated things.

She crossed her arms and fake-pouted, telling me, "You're no fun."

I poked her hard and she yelped. We got into a tickle fight then, but Wade broke us up. "Come on, now, guys; no roughhousing," he said. I was going to protest, but Ella pinched me on the arm and shook her head. I dropped it.

I shoved another cookie in my mouth to keep from saying anything else on the subject of boys, and shortly after, we were shooed out of the dining hall.

We were allowed to wander back up the mountain on our own or hang around the meadow and pavilion if we wanted. Since it was the first day, there was no Canteen, which was a bit of a disappointment.

Ella and I walked up to the meadow and lay on our backs on the soft grass, staring up at the sky. The sun wouldn't set for a while, since it was summertime, but the sky had already started to darken. A few stars peeked out, and the moon was rising. The grass smelled good; the air was mild. That high up in the mountains, it wasn't too hot, which was a blessing since I was still in my binder. A sense of peace settled over me. I was at camp, with my best friend. Nothing else could be better.

"Do you like it here so far?" Ella asked, after several long minutes of easy silence.

"I think so. I mean, it's not even been a whole day." I didn't want to think about the bathroom incident, so I put it out of my mind.

"I just want you to like it here. This is such a good place, with good people."

"Some of them, yeah."

"Oh, don't worry about them," she said, reading my mind. "They're losers and jerks. They wouldn't dare say anything to your face."

"I hope you're right."

"I usually am."

I stuck my tongue out at her, and she laughed. She had a lovely, musical laugh.

We settled into the comfortable silence we sometimes had with each other. Ella and I had been friends for so long we didn't need to talk all the time.

The other kids had started a Frisbee game around us, and there was much screaming and laughing. I could also hear the distinctive *whamp* of a basketball on concrete coming from the pavilion. The drone of cicadas almost drowned everything out, and a couple of fireflies buzzed by, their butts lighting up and disappearing.

Ella broke the silence. "Do you ever think it's weird that I don't like...anyone?"

I rolled over onto my side and frowned down at her. "What do you mean?"

"That I'm ace, you know, that I don't want to date anyone?"

"No, it's not weird. You know that."

She squirmed. "Yeah, I guess. But sometimes I wonder if I'm broken."

I grabbed her hand and squeezed it. "No, Ella, no. You're not broken. Don't think that." I felt doubly guilty for wishing she would just go out and get a boyfriend already.

"I just can't see myself...you know..." She looked away, her cheeks red.

"Did someone say something to you?"

She wouldn't meet my eyes, and I guessed I was right. "What happened?"

Still not looking at me, she blew her cheeks out. "I hate saying this, but I know I'm pretty. I get a lot of guys asking me out."

I knew that, too. Ella had long blonde hair that always seemed perfect. Her skin had never met a pimple, and when she wasn't out camping, she wore makeup like a supermodel. She was too pretty to be real, sometimes, but I didn't think of her that way. She was my sister, by choice if not by blood. I merely said, "Yeah, I know."

She looked at me then. "So a couple of guys have already asked me out. And I keep having to turn them down. It's exhausting. I hate doing it. Maybe I should say yes and get it over with?"

I was surprised they'd moved on her so quickly, but I didn't want to tell her that. It would only make her feel worse. So what I said was, "You mean, date? Or...?"

"No, not that. Just date. I mean, maybe I'll like it? Maybe I'm missing out? Maybe if I had a boyfriend, the rest will leave me alone?"

"You shouldn't date unless you really wanted to, Ella. Don't force yourself for someone else's sake."

"Well, no, it wouldn't be for someone else. It would be for me."

"I don't think it's a good idea, but if you think it will help..."

"Who do you think would be good for me?"

"Oh, please don't ask me to set you up." I groaned. I couldn't even get myself a date.

She shoved me, making me fall onto my back. "Hey!" I protested, but she pinned me down by sitting on me.

"Casey, come on. You know the boys in your cabin. Who would you want me to date?"

I squirmed, but Ella held me down easily. She was surprisingly strong, her legs muscular and powerful from being into soccer for so long.

"Who?" Ella barked.

We heard laughter from nearby, and she looked up and frowned. A group of kids had stopped playing Frisbee and were now staring at us.

To my horror, Gavin was there, laughing at me being pinned down by her.

"Problem, Casey?" asked Ryan, the guy with the attitude from my cabin. His face was stormy, his arms crossed over his chest.

Ella rolled off me and we stood hastily. I brushed myself off. "No problem," I said as casually as I could.

Ryan looked back and forth between us and then shook his head in disbelief. "I never thought a runt like you could get a girl like her." There was something else in his tone I didn't like, but I couldn't tell what it was.

"Fuck off," Ella said.

We all turned to her in surprise. I didn't often hear Ella swear. Her hands were clenched into fists.

"We're not..." I began.

"Looks like you two were making out, runt." Ryan said it to me, though he never took his eyes off of Ella. "You know that's against the rules, right?" His grin was full of malice.

Ella's jaw clenched, and my stomach did a flip-flop. "We were doing nothing of the sort," said Ella, flipping a lock of hair over her shoulder. "Not that what I do is any of your business anyway."

Ryan finally looked at me, but maybe only to look away from Ella. "Maybe Wade would like to know about this." He turned on his heel and went toward the tunnel of trees that led up to the cabins. The others, including Gavin, followed.

I moved to go after them, but Ella stopped me by grabbing my shoulder. "Don't," she said. "You'll never make it up there before him."

"Is there a shortcut?"

"Casey, drop it."

"What did he do to you?" I asked, realizing there must be history between the two of them. What else could explain Ryan's hostility?

"Nothing. Never mind." She wiped at her eyes, and I knew it could not be "nothing."

"Ella..."

"No!"

She turned and followed Ryan, leaving me there on the field with my jaw hanging open in shock.

What had just happened?

I didn't want to follow her right away. She clearly didn't want to talk to me, which hurt. So I walked around the field, and then jogged around it, to work off some of my anger. My binder made jogging uncomfortable, but right then I didn't care. I wheezed and slowed down, though.

Why would Ella have a history with Ryan? That question rolled around in my head the whole time I moved. Had they been together at camp before? Did Ryan like Ella, and was that why he instantly disliked me when he saw Ella and me together? And would Ryan succeed in getting us into trouble?

By the time I had calmed down enough to think straight, everyone else was heading back up the mountain. It was getting dark, and I didn't want to walk around without a flashlight, so I followed them. It was a long, hard trudge in the near darkness.

On my way, I noticed Alex was heading up at the same time. Again, he didn't look at me but somehow seemed aware of me, and I wondered what his problem was. He even stiffened as I drew near, and I veered away so I didn't disturb him.

At the top, the crowd was larger, but I could see people beginning to break up and go back to their cabins. The temperature was dropping too, and I shivered a bit. Summer nights in the mountains got chilly. I headed to my cabin, my breath heaving as much as I was able in my tight binder. It was starting to cut into my skin.

I ignored Ryan as I entered the cabin, but I could hear him laughing with a couple of the other boys. It hurt to see Gavin was one of them. Alex came in after me and went, stone-faced, to his bed. Without even taking off his clothes, he rolled over onto his side so his back was to everyone.

Okay. Cabin four didn't seem like the awesome place Wade was hoping it would be.

Luckily, the counselor heard Ryan say something unflattering about Ella and me and yelled at him. "That's not how cabin four boys talk!" he shouted, and I got a little satisfaction in seeing the dismay on Ryan's face.

But Wade didn't see the rude gesture Ryan made at him when he turned his back.

I figured Ryan's threat to tell on Ella and me was a bluff, because Wade never said anything about it. Ryan was sure to use it against us, though, and I wondered again what had happened between him and Ella.

I had other things to think about. Tonight would be the first test. I had to get undressed, and I wasn't about to go to the bathroom in the dark if I could help it. So I grabbed my clothes, hopped up onto my bed, and buried myself in the sheets.

Then, without being able to see what I was doing, I shimmied out of my dirty clothes and put on my pajamas. I had to remove the binder, too, which I absolutely hated doing, but I couldn't sleep in it. It could seriously hurt my ribs or my lungs if I wore it too long, and I'd been in it all day. It was hard to get off, especially both lying down and trying not to be noticed, and I wrestled with it and hoped no one saw.

Unfortunately for me, they had. Ryan was pointing and laughing at me, but not out loud, since Wade was still around. The counselor had settled onto his own bunk and wasn't paying attention to anything.

I ignored Ryan and balled the binder up in my dirty clothes. My pajamas were baggy enough to cover the bulges on my chest, but I was still self-conscious about them. I folded my arms across my chest, pinning my breasts down, and packed away my things as quickly as I could with my arms as close to my body as I could get them. Then I went to Wade's bunk and whispered, "Can we talk for a second?"

He eyed me and then nodded. "We can walk to the bathroom."

Relief flooded me. I needed to go, but hadn't wanted to go alone, not again. And that gave me a good excuse to bring up what had happened. He grabbed a flashlight, and I followed him out of the cabin and into the cool night.

"What's up?" he asked quietly.

"I had an encounter in the bathroom," I said, and then explained it. "Someone told one of the kids I'm trans. Maybe not actually me, but someone let it slip there was a trans kid at camp."

Wade's brow had furrowed, and his dark lips were pressed into a tight line. "I'm sorry, Casey, that you had to hear that. I can see if we can find out anything, but since you didn't see them, it'll be hard to get any answers."

"I know. I just...I just wanted to talk to someone about it. I mean, should I tell people I'm trans, to prevent awkward questions later?"

"What do you mean?"

"If people know, then if someone tries to out me, they won't be able to use it against me. If it's a surprise, more people could be upset about it." And accuse me of being a liar, a cheater, a deceitful person. It had happened before at my old school.

"I'll talk to the director and see what he says. For now, don't worry about it okay? But if you want someone to go with you into the bathrooms..."

"No, that's okay." That offer always felt weird to me. It would make me stand out. No one else needed a guard in the bathroom, why should I? It felt creepy, but I did appreciate the gesture.

We went into the bathroom, and there were a few other boys in there. Luckily, I didn't have to wait for a stall, so I went in and did my business. Wade still finished before me, though, and he waited for me outside.

The walk back was silent, but before we got to the cabin, he stopped me and said, "I'm sorry about Ryan. I had actually petitioned for him not to be allowed in my cabin. He's a known troublemaker."

"So why is he allowed in? Don't they throw people out who break the rules?"

"I wish it was that simple," Wade said, sighing. "Ryan is the camp owner's nephew."

Well, shit.

I wondered if that was why Ella hadn't wanted to talk about him and figured it probably was.

"Thanks for letting me know."

"He's a bully, but he's not so bright. Just stay away from him as much as you can, and I'll try to watch out for you."

It was going to be hard to stay away from him when he was only a bunk away. "You know he doesn't like you much?"

Wade rolled his eyes, and I laughed as he clutched at his heart, pretending to be mortally wounded. "How will I survive?" he said, stumbling.

He then clapped me on the shoulder, and we went the rest of the way back to the cabin.

The boys had gotten rowdy since Wade had been gone, but they quieted down as soon as he shouted at them.

"Lights-out in fifteen, boys," he said.

I climbed back into my bunk and pulled out my book.

Wade turned out the light when it was time, and I settled down to try to sleep.

It had been an okay day. I'd hoped it would be better, but at least so far I hadn't been outed. That was all I could hope for.

The last thing I thought of before I fell asleep was that I hadn't even showered yet.

Chapter Two

WADE SHOOK US all awake in the morning. "Get up! Time to clean the cabin!" he chirped, far too happy for the morning.

I groaned and growled at him as he shook my leg. I did not like mornings, and chipper morning people made me like mornings even less. But I got up and grabbed my clothes. I went to the bathroom to shower and dress, and it took several long minutes to struggle into my binder while I was still damp. No one saw me, though, which was what counted.

I hurriedly finished changing and ran back up to the cabin, so as not to be seen as slacking. It was my turn to sweep, so I made my bed and then chased everyone out once they were done so I could pass the broom over the floorboards. I did as good a job as I could, even getting into the corners.

Once I had finished, the other boys came in and completed the other chores. There was making the beds, tapping the bugs out of the screen windows, mopping the floor, and dusting. Outside, we cleared the path to the door (rocks tended to roll down from the mountain). In addition, each cabin pair was given a community chore to do. We lucked out and didn't have one for the first day, which meant the cabin itself was going to have to be spotless. Wade had us even reline the road outside of the cabin with rocks, since they tended to migrate as kids tripped over them or deliberately kicked them around.

Wade looked over everything and deemed it acceptable. Finished with chores, we lined up with the other cabins to go down to breakfast.

As before, once we were down at the dining hall, I slipped in to sit beside Ella. She was looking a little wan that morning, with red around her eyes. Lily wasn't sitting next to her.

"Hey," I said, bumping her arm so she'd look at me.

Her smile was tight, but at least she smiled at me. I decided not to press her about it. If she was upset, she would tell me why eventually, but not until she was ready. I wondered if it had anything to do with Ryan.

Breakfast was pancakes with tons of butter and maple syrup. There was even fruit compote, which was still warm. I inhaled three large pancakes, and that made Ella laugh a little. "You eat like a teenage boy," she muttered at me.

"That's because I am!" I winked at her, and she laughed again. That was better.

Conversation picked up after that, but neither of us could share confidential news with so many other people around. So we talked about the weird dreams we'd both had that night and about the activities planned for the day.

At the end of breakfast, Lars, the gorgeous counselor, stood up and had some announcements. His voice was deep and pleasant but slow, and I found myself wondering what he looked like under the loud Christmas sweater he was wearing. He didn't seem to see any of us, staring off into the distance instead. "Some of you may know what I'm about to announce," he said, "and some of you won't. But, that's okay! This is to tell you that at every session we have a talent show. Winners get bragging rights and pizza! Signups will start this afternoon, but the show won't be until next week."

Ella poked me. "You should do it!"

"Why?" I asked.

"Because you're a good singer!"

"No way," I said. I didn't want that much attention focused on me. My singing wasn't that great, anyway. Plus, I didn't want to pursue it any further until I started testosterone. Who knew what my voice would sound like when it dropped?

After, we were free to go to our morning activities.

The compass group was to meet in the field, so Ella and I went back up the road. The dodgeball group was already forming under the pavilion, and the football people had staked out a large section of the field.

Two counselors stood next to a pile of compasses on the far side of the field. Ella waved happily to one and said, "That's Annabelle; she's my counselor."

Annabelle was plain and pale but had a bubbly personality. Her hair was mousy brown, and her eyes were hidden behind glasses. The other counselor's name tag said, "Rich, Cabin Two." He was short and stocky, with a shaved head and bright blue eyes. He stood with his hands on his hips, looking like he was distinctly uncomfortable.

Only a few people had signed up for the compass training, far fewer than they could have accommodated. I was kind of glad.

We spent a good portion of the morning learning all about compasses. Rich marched us all over the field and the sparse woods just next to it, barking out orders on how to follow with our compasses. Once satisfied we knew enough, Annabelle and Rich blindfolded us and led us into the woods. We were given directions on how to find our way back, but that was it.

I happily tromped through the forest alone, hoping Ella wasn't too upset about it. She hated being by herself if she could help it.

I easily made it back to the field. Ella wasn't long after me, and she hugged me. "Help me get the sticks out of my hair," she said as she let me go.

She didn't have many, but I helped her anyway, because I knew she needed the reassurance of touch.

We didn't need to wait to see when the others returned, so we wandered off. "Let's go watch the dodgeball game!" she said.

I wasn't entirely thrilled with the idea, but she had signed up to do the compass activity with me, so I relented. There was a crowd of shrieking and laughing kids under the pavilion, throwing large red balls at each other.

Luckily for me, we hadn't ever played dodgeball in school. Because of its bad reputation, it had been banned in my district. I knew about it of course, because I'd seen TV shows and movies with it. The geeky or queer kids always got picked on by the jocks, har har. At my old school, I was sure that was how it would have gone, but not at my new school.

Still, I wasn't eagerly looking forward to playing it. What if someone hit me in the chest? Physical activities weren't entirely fun with a binder on, either.

We sat on the grass near the pavilion and watched. Ella explained it to me. It seemed complicated, and I only half listened, still not sure I would ever want to play it.

We watched for a while longer, and I had to reluctantly admit it looked like fun. "We'll do that next time," I said. Ella hugged me—of course, she did.

Eventually we got bored with watching, but it wasn't yet time for lunch. Ella suggested joining in, but I didn't want to do that. I didn't want to be on opposing teams, and the numbers would be uneven if we joined only one. So we went back up to the lodge to hang out.

Washington Lodge was nearly empty, with only a few couples and clumps of friends talking and wasting time. I pulled Ella into a corner and sat her down. "Now, tell me what's up." It was time she told me.

She blew her hair out of her eyes and looked away. "Okay, I'll tell you." Ella took a deep breath and went on. "Two years ago, Ryan and I kind of dated. We were the first for each other; neither of us had dated before. It was just here," she hastily added when I looked skeptical. I'd never heard of her dating anyone before. I was surprised she hadn't told me about it, and I wondered why.

Ella went on. "That was how I found out I was aro and ace. I didn't like dating. It felt weird. I didn't like how Ryan was so possessive of me. He always wanted to touch me when I didn't want to be touched."

That was saying something, for Ella.

"I mean, we were only twelve, and he kept talking about us getting married and having kids." She shuddered. "I thought at first I was asexual because of him. But I couldn't bring myself to date anyone else, either. The thought of sex? I just can't see myself doing that with anyone." She took a big breath and said in a rush, "He tried to ask me out again already this year. I had to be really firm with him, and he didn't like it. He was pretty rude about it."

I couldn't relate to her asexuality, but Ella was my friend, and I tried to empathize with her as best I could. "I'm sorry, Ella. He seems like such a creep. But even if it is just because of him, so what? Maybe you're just not ready to date?" I hated saying that to her, because asexual people got the "you haven't found the right person yet" crap all the time. That wasn't what I was telling her, and I hoped she got the difference.

"Maybe," she said, looking away again. "Will I ever be ready?"

"That doesn't matter," I told her. "There's nothing wrong with being ace, Ella. If you find someone, great. If not, great."

She smiled at me, and it was a little watery. I drew her into a hug. "Love you," I told her, and she knew how I meant it.

"Love you, too."

There was a commotion as we pulled apart, and I saw Alex had knocked over a bench. I hadn't even seen him come in, but he hastily left, a huge scowl on his face and his hands curled into fists. The other kids were eyeing each other amusedly, and I wondered what they'd said to him. Had they done something mean? I frowned at them, but none of them looked guilty.

We went outside to do something to get our minds off of Ryan. Ella wanted to show me her cabin, but boys weren't allowed in. She did stand in the door and let me peek in, much to the consternation of the girls inside. We laughed about it, and I did the same for her at my cabin, but none of the boys were there.

"They all look the same," she said.

On our walk, we spotted Lars in another loud pink sweater, that time with an Easter theme. He was also wearing a long flowing skirt, which flapped around his hairy legs and hiking boots whenever he strode back and forth across the grounds.

The boys laughed at him behind his back, but he either took no notice or didn't care. The girls didn't know what to make of him. He was so gorgeous most of them drooled over him, but I think his dress sense weirded them out.

I thought that was silly, but cis people tended to be silly sometimes about gender expression. I didn't mind pink, but I'd never wear it, not wanting to deal with the fallout of being a trans boy in something considered feminine. Lars didn't seem to mind the color, and he seemed like he was enjoying the skirt.

I thought he was brilliant.

People should be allowed to wear whatever they wanted, whenever they wanted. Lars looked good in a dress, but he'd probably look good in a burlap sack.

Ella and I wasted more time just wandering and talking until we had to go down the mountain for lunch. We went back to our respective cabins to meet the counselors, who counted us and herded us to our spots.

While we were waiting, I noticed Alex looked, if it were possible, even more morose than usual. I didn't know him well, but he didn't seem to have any other friends that I could see. He stood off to one side, as far away from the rest of the cabin as he could get and still be in the right place.

I don't really know why, but I went over to him and said, "Hey, are you okay?"

He didn't look at me, but said, "I'm fine."

"Anything you want to talk about?"

He looked at me then, but his facial expression didn't change. "No, I'm fine." His jaw tightened as he looked away, glaring at the trees.

"Okay," I said and wandered away again. I guess he didn't want any friends, which was sad.

I ate with Ella again, and we were joined by both Lily and her brother, Nick. I wasn't too sure about Nick, since he was one of the ones standing around when Ryan had been laughing at me. I was cool to him until he said, as he passed me the rolls, "Sorry, man, about yesterday. Ryan was way off base." He bobbled his head in a strange sort of shrug. "Ryan's an ass, but you know..."

"It's okay," I said, relieved, but also not wanting to hear why he still hung around someone like Ryan.

Lunch was fried chicken, and as promised, it was very good. We also had cornbread, which I detested, and collard greens. More cookies were served for dessert, but of a different variety than we had before. We also had fruit, and as much bug juice as I could swallow.

Nick played a lot of video games but was into all sorts of geeky and nerdy things. He even cosplayed and explained that he was one of the youngest winners ever in a national costume contest.

"Wow," I said, impressed. "What character?"

He named one I wasn't familiar with, and he lamented, "If we had cell phone service up here, I could show you pictures."

"Yeah, that'd be great!"

Lily didn't cosplay but was the brains behind Nick's costuming wins. "I do all the mechanical stuff," she explained in between bites of cookie. "Like making his chest piece glow, and the wings actually work. They're hydraulic."

"I can't wait to see this," I told him.

We talked more about cosplay, which I had only a passing interest in, since I couldn't sew. But I'd been to the local comic conventions and had enjoyed most of the games and comics that cosplayers emulated. I was always impressed by the costumes.

At the end of lunch, one of the other out-of-cabin-counselors, a tall Indian woman named Ritika, stood up and said, "We're going to announce the Clean Cabin Award!"

The hall quieted down, and we all eagerly awaited the news. While I didn't care much about soda, I was hoping our hard work would be noticed.

"Everyone's cabin looked really good," she said, smiling. "But it's only the first day! Make sure you keep working hard. The first Clean Cabin Award goes to cabin three!"

We clapped politely while they celebrated, cheering and hugging. Ritika continued, "After lunch is Quiet Time, but before you go to your cabins, make sure to sign up for your afternoon events."

Once the rest of the announcements were done, Ella said, "Cabin three also gets to go to the showers during Quiet Time." She made a face and sniffed at herself.

"Can anyone go during Quiet Time?" I thought of my hurried morning shower and how inconvenient that was going to be.

"No," Ella said. "And the rush is right after. We have some free time between then and activities and dinner, and everyone tries to shower then."

"I might try showering before bed then," I said.

"It gets cold. Better try it when the sun is up."

I didn't say it out loud, but it was going to be better for me to shower when no one was around. If I could do everything, including getting dressed, in the shower, that would be ideal. I preferred to do that as far away from other people as possible.

Once more, we trooped up the mountain. I signed up for dodgeball for the afternoon because Ella really wanted to play instead of watch. In the cabin, Wade was already telling the other boys what we could and could not do during Quiet Time. "You can nap, which I highly recommend, or you can read or do something else quietly. You just can't go to the showers, and you can't make a lot of noise. No talking, okay?"

I didn't think nap time was a useful way to spend part of an afternoon, but I could see some of the others were tired. I hopped onto my bunk with my book and read for the hour.

Once it was over, everyone else headed for the showers. I pulled Wade aside and asked him if it was okay if I showered at night.

"As long as you're in bed by lights-out," he said.

Good, because that would be the best thing for me. I wouldn't run the risk of encountering anyone else in the showers. I might get cold, but that was an easy price to pay. I hoped no one took special notice of me going to the showers at night.

I changed into some clothes that would do better for dodgeball and met Ella at Lincoln Lodge. I hoped I wasn't going to regret this.

A crowd had already formed when we got to the pavilion. To my dismay, Ryan was there. Alex was, too, but he was standing off to the side, ignoring everyone else. I wondered why he'd signed up if he didn't like anyone. Being hit by large balls probably wasn't going to help his mood or what he thought of everyone.

I was surprised to see Lars was one of the counselors in charge. Wade was the other, which was a relief. If anything went badly between Ryan and me, he'd be there to see it. If he was paying attention.

Lars had changed clothes yet again and was now wearing a pair of bell-bottoms that looked like they were originally from the '70s. They were worn and faded and had a riot of brightly colored patches all over them. He was still wearing the ugly Easter sweater and hadn't even broken a sweat despite the heat.

Weird guy.

I couldn't help but notice his rear end in the tight jeans, though.

Ella elbowed me. "You're being obvious," she whispered. "But I don't blame you. You know we joke that the butt buns were modeled by Lars, right?"

I blushed so furiously my face got hot enough to spring out in an immediate sweat. Ella was smart enough not to laugh at me.

Wade split us into two teams, and he wisely put Ella, Ryan, and me on the same team. Alex, too, which seemed to cheer him up a bit. Being on the same team meant Ryan wouldn't have a chance or reason to hit me with a ball. But I caught the expression on Ella's face. She stood as far away from him as she could, and I saw him glance at her a few times.

We spread out over the pavilion, and I stood toward the back with Ella and Alex. I didn't know how vicious this was going to be and didn't want to get hit first if I could help it.

Both Lars and Wade threw a ball, one to each team, and it all began.

Two teams opposed one another across the centerline, and with two balls, it would be harder to keep track of them both. Once hit with a ball, instead of being "out," a player would go to "jail," which was on the fringes of the opposing side's space. To get free of jail, they'd have to hit someone else.

I liked that one hit didn't mean you were out of the game entirely. And with two balls it was harder for the teams to monitor who had one, and so the kids in jail got out pretty quickly.

Even though it was difficult following both balls, I couldn't help but smile as I bobbed and weaved as they were chucked at me. Ella got hit early on and jogged over to the jail on the other side. I tried my best to get her a ball, but I had a hard time catching them.

The binder made running harder, and I was almost constantly out of breath, but that was okay. I dodged another ball, only to have it bounce off the cement and take Alex in the gut. He *oofed* and then stalked off to the jail.

I ran after the ball and got it before it rolled into our jail, and chucked it at Ella. She caught it and immediately hurled it at an unsuspecting player on the other side. It grazed his arm, and Ella yelped with glee. She ran back over, and we high-fived.

Our side didn't seem to be doing as well, but that hardly mattered.

Only moments after Ella got out, I got hit and went into jail. Alex stood near me, but his mind clearly wasn't on the game. He stared off into the woods for a while, and I wondered why.

I got the ball that Ryan—of all people—threw at me but missed my shot. The ball rolled over to the other side, where no one was standing. I wasn't going to make it, so I nudged Alex. "Go! You can catch it."

He eyed me with disdain and didn't move.

Okay, then.

Someone on the other team got the ball and chucked it. Two balls at the same time went for Ryan, but he was too fast. He caught one of them and hurled it back at me. That time, I handed the ball to Alex instead. "Go for it."

He took it, surprise evident on his face. A girl turned her back to keep track of the other ball, and Alex nailed her with his. She shrieked in mock anger, and then, grinning, gave him a thumbs-up and trotted over to the jail. Alex looked at me, said a quick "Thanks," and went back to our side.

I spent the next five minutes in jail, trying to get someone to throw me a ball. But they were either intercepted or when I got the ball I missed my target.

After, I gave up trying and just watched, hoping someone would throw one my way. But in jail I stayed until Lars and Wade finally called the game to a halt.

We were all sweaty and tired and out of breath. I wanted to take my binder off, since it was soaked and uncomfortable, but I couldn't take a shower yet. The binder was so tight, I shouldn't be wearing it so much anyway, but I didn't know of a good time to take it off and not have my chest noticed. It should have come off at Quiet Time, but I hadn't had the chance.

It was exhausting. I was about ready to tell everyone anyway, just so I could stop bending over backward to hide it.

One of the balls got away from Lars and rolled to my feet. As I bent down to pick it up, Ryan walked up to me. I was about to straighten up and thank him for the assists, but he veered into me and knocked me over. Since I was still mostly bent over, I went face-first into the concrete, scraping my cheek.

"Hey, asshole!" I yelled from the floor, my hand held to my stinging face.

A few people stopped talking to stare. Ryan turned to me and fury was on his face. "What of it, runt?"

A red haze filled my vision. My heart pounded in my chest. I was sure he knew, and he was going to blurt it out in front of everyone.

"Why help him, anyway?" Ryan scoffed, jerking his head at someone. I looked at who he was referring to and was surprised to see it was Alex. What problem did Ryan have with Alex?

"It's just a game," I said, standing up. "Why the hell would you push me over?"

"He's gay," Ryan said, and then repeated it, mocking, "Gaaaayyy."

I flushed.

"Hey, hey now," said Wade, noticing the brewing fight. He saw my bloodied cheek. "Are you all right?"

"Fine," I said.

"What happened?"

Ella cut in, "Ryan pushed Casey!" Her blonde hair swung around her face as she pointed an accusing finger at him.

Wade turned a dark look on Ryan, who shrugged, smiled a shit-eating grin, and said, "It was an accident."

"Like hell it was," I said.

Wade frowned at both of us. "None of that," he said, shaking a finger at me.

"What?" I asked, honestly confused. "What did I do?"

Wade ignored me. "Shake hands, both of you."

"No way," I blurted. "He pushed me."

"It was an accident!"

"Then apologize!" I yelled back.

Wade smacked a fist into his palm. "Enough! Both of you will be doing extra chores for fighting!"

I opened my mouth to protest, and Ella made an outraged sound, but Wade said, "Not another word out of any of you! Now, we've had a nice round of dodgeball, and this is what's going to happen." He turned to me. "Casey, go to the nurse and get that checked out. Ryan, go back to the cabin. You're there until dinner." He shook his finger in Ryan's rebellious face. "I'll be up in a few minutes, so you'd better be there."

Ryan stormed off, trailed by a few of his hangers-on.

Ella took my arm and fiercely said, "I'll go with you to the nurse."

I glared after Ryan, wishing I had lasers for eyes so I could burn a hole in his back. My cheek smarted. Ella led me off the pavilion and across the field.

There was a tiny house next to the field, across the road, which I hadn't really paid attention to. It turned out it was the nurse's place.

Ella knocked on the door, and an elderly woman in a long blue skirt and white blouse opened the door. "Oh, dear," she said, noticing my bloody cheek.

She sent Ella back out, with strict instructions to let Wade know where I was, and drew me into her examination room. "What happened?" she asked.

"Another kid pushed me, and I fell onto the concrete." My anger had started to fade, and the injustice of it was starting to rankle. Why were adults so oblivious and unfair?

"Well, that's a problem." She bustled around the room, getting a bottle of hydrogen peroxide, some cotton swabs, and a packet of gauze bandages and tape from a few cupboards and drawers. She poured out some of the peroxide onto a piece of gauze and dabbed at my cheek. It stung worse, and I winced.

"Looks pretty clean," she said after a moment. "That's a good thing. But I'll still give you something to numb it up a bit."

She got out a tube of something from another drawer, squeezed some out onto a swab, and dabbed it onto my face. It was cool, and the stinging subsided as she worked.

The nurse put a large piece of gauze over the wound, and then taped it up. It covered almost half my face. "There you go."

"Can I use your bathroom?" I asked.

"Of course."

She showed me where it was, and I took the opportunity to remove my binder. It had started to smell, and I felt gross. But the pressure was off of my chest. My ribs were hurting, and that wasn't a good sign. Big red creases marred my skin, and I checked them carefully for bleeding. The binder hadn't cut me but had come pretty close. I might have to forgo it for a day, and that wasn't a great option. I knew I couldn't wear it for at least the rest of the afternoon. I shoved it into my pocket as best I could, though it left a big lump there.

I left the infirmary after thanking the nurse and trudged my way back up the mountain. My face still stung a little, though the ointment she'd put on was starting to work. I went straight to the cabin and found Wade railing at Ryan. That gave me a little bit of satisfaction, until the counselor rounded on me as well.

"I'm disappointed in both of you." Wade glanced back and forth between us. "I can't believe I have two boys from my cabin in trouble for fighting. I've never had a situation like this."

The anger inside me rose, and I tried to tell him I didn't start it, but he never gave me a chance to speak.

"I don't care whose fault it is, or who started it." His voice rose to drown me out. "This is unacceptable. Both of you will be working extra to make up for this, and I might have you do it the whole rest of the time you're here. I clearly outlined the rules ahead of time, and you broke the most important one on the first full day. I don't want to hear it!" he said as I opened my mouth again. Ryan was staring at the wall, his face frozen. "If I found out either of you have taken one more step out of line, I'm going to call your families and have them come pick you up. Is that clear?"

My heart sank.

Ryan sneered, but Wade wasn't going to have any of it. "You attacked another camper, Ryan, and even your uncle and your dad will pull you out for that."

That wiped the expression of off Ryan's face, and his jaw tightened, his lips a thin white line. But he said nothing.

"Both of you are to stay here until dinner. To make sure you don't get into any more trouble, I'm staying here, too. There will be no more talking."

I stormed to my bunk, kicked open my trunk, and pulled my binder out of my pocket when no one was looking and dumped it there. Grabbing my book, I thought reading might help, but all I could do was stare at the page and imagine punching Ryan in the face. I repeatedly went over what I wanted to say to Wade but hadn't been allowed. None of it was nice.

It was totally unfair I was getting punished. I hadn't done anything to Ryan, and he had knocked me over. And that was after he'd actually helped me in the game.

His words, though, about his reasoning behind the sudden change, came back to me. I had almost forgotten them in the chaos.

Ryan had claimed that Alex was gay. I had helped get Alex out of jail, and that apparently offended Ryan enough for him to attack me.

If that were true, it was no wonder Alex was cold and distant. Especially if he knew Ryan was prejudiced, or maybe he'd done something to him before.

I might be able to reach out to Alex if he would let me. But I had to be careful. If he really was gay, he might be sensitive about it and wouldn't like me talking about it around him. If he wasn't gay, he might blow up and do something to prove he wasn't—like fight me. I couldn't get caught fighting again.

I slammed my book down and stared at the ceiling instead. Why did we all have to be so stupid to one another? Why couldn't we just accept one another the way we were? Why did I have to fight so hard to be myself? Why should Alex have to hide whether he was gay or not?

I rolled over and looked out the screen window, feeling the cooler air blow on my face. It was getting close to dinnertime, and the sun was already starting to descend. My stomach growled.

I felt sorry for Alex. I felt sorry for myself. I even, sort of, felt sorry for Ryan. It must be exhausting to carry around all that hate, that tension, inside him. But I couldn't feel too sorry for him. He'd chosen that, and he could choose not to hate if he wanted to.

There were kids playing and running around outside, enjoying themselves, and sadness crept into my heart, replacing the anger. I should be out there, too, with Ella, having fun. Instead, I was only watching it all, and it was just the first day. I wanted to hate this place. A sudden homesickness overwhelmed me, and I almost rolled over and told Wade to call my parents. I was leaving.

But I couldn't do that. I couldn't let Ryan win—let him chase me away from something I'd wanted to do for years. I was living as a boy, passing as a boy. Even getting into trouble as a boy. It was what I'd wanted for so long. I couldn't give up now. I couldn't disappoint Ella, either, who had wanted me to come to this camp so badly.

Next year, there'd be no more camp for me. I'd be fifteen and in high school, too old to go to camp again. I didn't want the memories of my first time at a regular camp to be tainted by me leaving before I'd even gotten through an entire day.

I didn't want to disappoint myself, my parents, or Ella that way.

I watched the kids outside until dinnertime when Wade sullenly shooed us out of the cabin to line up. Once more, Alex was off to one side by himself, his shoulders hunched over, kicking gloomily at rocks. I could hear the others whispering about him, too. Word had spread after what Ryan had said at the pavilion.

Their whispers worried me. If they did that because Alex might be gay, what would they say behind my back if they found out I was trans?

I threw caution to the wind and walked right up to him and said, "Sorry I didn't get you out of jail sooner."

He looked at me, his brow furrowed as though he couldn't understand why I was talking to him. I ignored it and went on.

"It was a fun game anyway. I haven't ever played it before."

He eyed me and said nothing.

"Have you ever played Greek dodgeball before?"

"No." His voice was cold, but his face had softened a little.

"Did you like it?"

He shrugged. "I guess."

"Too bad I couldn't get out of jail at the end, though," I said, making light of it. "Maybe next time."

He nodded, but then it was time to walk down. He sped up, so it was hard for me to keep up. I decided to let it go. Maybe he was just that shy, and showing him I was harmless would help.

I walked alone down the mountain, until we'd nearly reached the field and pavilion. Then, to my surprise, Gavin sidled up next to me and leaned over. "Hey," he said quietly.

Shocked, I stared at him. "What's up?"

"Just wanted to apologize. Ryan was way out of line. I thought it was funny at first, but he went too far. I'm sorry he got you into trouble."

"Thanks," I said, forcing the word out around my heart, which had suddenly lodged itself in my throat. He had pretty blue eyes.

He smiled at me, and then went on ahead, walking faster than I wanted to. Without a bra or my binder, walking too fast made me bounce, which was uncomfortable. I'd brought a sports bra, for just this sort of thing, but hadn't gotten a chance to put it on. Besides, I hated it. It set off my dysphoria something fierce, and I hadn't wanted to bother with it because of that. Already feeling pretty bad, I didn't need a dysphoria attack on top of everything.

Dinner was tasty lasagna with salad. As usual, I sat with Ella. Shocking us all, Gavin asked if he could join us, and when I wasn't able to respond, Ella had to answer.

"Please sit!" She grinned and squeezed my leg under the table as I fought to keep the blush off of my face.

"Thanks!" Gavin slid into the seat next to me, and Lily and Nick sat across from us.

Gavin was very polite, and we talked about *Pioneers of Noran* until Lily and Ella got bored enough to start into their own subject. Nick was quiet but listened intently to the two of us geeking out over our favorite game.

By the end of dinner, I had completely forgotten my previous depression. Things were looking up. I had friends in Ella and Nick, and even Lily. And now, Gavin, my crush, was paying attention to me. And he was actually nice, once he was away from Ryan.

Dessert was fruit, and I muttered how I missed the cookies.

"Can't have them all the time," Gavin said, and he nudged my shoulder.

My heart sped up at the touch, and even though his hand had only brushed my shoulder, I imagined I could still feel his fingers there, a ghostly trace. My arm tingled.

Ella was practically bouncing up and down in her seat, and I had to give her a look to calm her down, lest she give it away. I didn't want Gavin to know I liked him.

Two years ago, just as I was beginning to realize I was a boy, I had crushed on another boy really hard. I'd only just cut my hair and started dressing more like a boy. I hadn't yet changed my name or even come out to anyone, but everyone knew something was up—that I was different. When I managed to gather my courage and ask him out, the boy had gotten offended and made a scene where he publicly begged me not to like him.

It had been mortifying and devastating. That was one of the main reasons I wasn't all that interested in finding love any time soon, especially not here. But I couldn't help the crush.

Besides, it was hard enough being trans, but add queer on top of it, and it made dating almost impossible.

After dinner, we'd have Canteen, of course, which meant socializing and soda. I wasn't interested in the soda, but Gavin seemed particularly enthusiastic, so I pulled up my own excitement in response. We went back up the mountain as soon as we were allowed.

Cabin three, who had won the Clean Cabin Award, got to be in line first. But the three of us, Ella, Gavin, and I, were next. We got our sodas, and still Gavin stayed with us instead of going to hang out with the rest of cabin four.

When we sat down on the stone wall outside the Lincoln Lodge, I had to ask, "So, what's up with them?" The other cabin four boys were hanging out together, lounging on the rocks in front of cabin seven, and I waved my soda can in their direction. "Why aren't you hanging out with them?"

"Did you want me to?" Gavin asked.

"No," I said quickly, "I just wasn't sure why you suddenly dropped them." Why was I saying this? Did I want to drive him away?

He shrugged, and I was relieved he didn't take it personally. "I got tired of their crap. They're not really nice, you know?" He nodded his head as Alex walked by, and the other group of boys got quiet and watched him walk past with amusement on their faces. Alex was ignoring them, but they laughed and made lewd gestures as he passed. "See? I just don't think that's cool."

"No, it's not," I agreed.

"I thought you guys would be cooler, you know, since you like *Pioneers* so much."

Ella cut in, "Well, some of us." She rolled her eyes and then winked, and we laughed. I stuck my tongue out at her.

"Well, some of us have better taste," I said. She pretended to be offended, and we all dissolved into giggles again.

We hung out that night, laughing and getting to know one another. I flirted as best I could with Gavin but wasn't very skilled at it and held back because I didn't want to be too obvious. But I used any excuse to touch him, and he didn't seem to mind. By the end of the evening, we were sitting close enough our legs almost touched. He didn't move away.

After my lonely shower that night, I went to bed, but it was hard to get to sleep. I kept thinking about the one time Gavin had touched my arm, about how close we'd been all night. And he was below me right now, lightly snoring. His closeness was so distracting, my feelings intensifying at the thought of how near he was. I eventually did go to sleep, the sound of Gavin breathing lulling me into my dreams.

Chapter Three

THE NEXT MORNING, after completing my assigned cabin chore (mopping after Alex had swept), Wade delivered me to the latrines to help out cabins two and seven. There was a lot of chuckling and whispering behind my back, but I ignored them. At least I was cleaning the boys' bathroom and not the girls'. I tried to find some sort of silver lining in all this.

What made everything even worse was that I couldn't wear my binder. My ribs still ached, and my sternum hurt from the day before. I could hurt myself more if I wore it again. So I'd put on the baggiest shirt I had and hunched my shoulders, hoping that would be enough. The sports bra underneath was a size too small but still didn't offer much in terms of concealment. It was better than nothing.

My face still stung, too, but when I removed the bandage there wasn't anything more than a regular scrape. Nothing bad, so I declined to go back to the nurse to have it checked out again. Wade seemed to think it was fine, too. Part of me wished it was worse, so maybe he'd punish Ryan more and let me off the hook. No such luck.

At breakfast—waffles with fruit compote—Ella seemed a little faded around the edges. I asked if she was okay, and she threw her usual smile at me. But I could see in her eyes that she didn't have her whole heart in it.

"I'm fine," she said when I opened my mouth to press. I closed it and didn't pry, wondering if this still had something to do with Ryan.

A pool party was announced for that night. Instead of afternoon activities, we would have an extended Quiet Time and then an early dinner to accommodate it. There would be even more food at the party.

There was an air of excitement as we all trooped back up the mountain for our morning activities. By mutual agreement, Ella and I had decided against dodgeball again. I didn't want to do anything physical without being able to wear a binder, and for fear that Ryan would be there to make it worse. Otherwise, I'd be too self-conscious and uncomfortable, and the sports bra could only do so much. So we signed up for friendship bracelets, as boring as it sounded.

Surprisingly, so did Gavin.

One of the female counselors was there to teach us how to knot the bright string into fun designs. I was hopeless at it, but Ella's knots were tiny and perfect, and her bracelets more intricate than the counselor's. She even showed us a few patterns the counselor didn't know.

Gavin was clumsy at it, but it gave me an excuse to touch his hands as I helped him knot. I wasn't that much better, but Ella flat-out refused to help him, saying she was much too busy with her own bracelet. Her lips twitched from keeping back a knowing, triumphant smile.

At one point, Gavin had managed to get the string wrapped around his hands so badly he couldn't get them out without making a huge tangle.

"Here, let me get it" I leaned over and grabbed both of his hands, sliding right up next to him. His leg and shoulder pressed against mine, and I could feel the heat building in my face. He was so close I could see the bright red lashes on his cheeks as he looked down at his hands. He had a super large, very dark freckle directly under his right eye, and it was adorable.

I slid a hand down his arm and took the string from his fingers. He looked at me, and we were almost close enough to kiss. I think I stopped breathing when he smiled at me. "Like this?" he asked, as he slid his hand into mine.

I froze, my heart hammering so hard I was afraid he'd be able to see it slamming against my ribs. "Yeah," I gasped out. It sounded too breathy, too intimate, even to me. I hoped he didn't notice. Or maybe I did want him to notice.

Gavin pulled his hands away, and the moment was broken. He had untangled himself with a deft move, both from the string and from me. It had been too intimate, then. I had pushed too far, too fast.

He stood up abruptly, and I hastily shifted over, as though what we had just done hadn't meant anything to me.

But there was a bright red flush creeping up his pale skin, drowning out his freckles one by one. "I, uh, gotta go," he mumbled. He left quickly.

Ella, oblivious to the awkwardness, giggled and reached over to squeeze my hand. "That went well?" she asked, with one raised eyebrow.

"Maybe." I took a deep breath to calm myself. He had seemed pretty embarrassed by it, though.

I spent the rest of the morning agonizing over whether Gavin could be gay or bisexual. Had he distanced himself from Ryan because of his remark about Alex? Was he queer and didn't like Ryan making fun of it? Or was he still not sure, and I had just opened his eyes with same-sex attraction?

I also tried not to make it all about me. What if Gavin was straight, and he was picking up that I was assigned female at birth? I wanted him to like me as a boy, not as a girl.

When we were alone, I badgered Ella about my appearance. "Am I still passing?" I asked her, flattening out my T-shirt and hoping my chest wasn't too obvious. Without the binder, it seemed horrifyingly apparent I had breasts. They weren't big, but they were impossible to miss in some of my clothing. The sports bra didn't do much to hide the telltale lumps under my shirt.

"You're fine," she told me, more than once.

"Are you sure? You're not just being nice?"

Exasperated, she rolled her eyes. "You look like you always do, Casey. Like a boy. Now stop worrying! I think he does like you!"

At lunch, it was announced that cabin eight had won the Clean Cabin Award, which was disappointing. I was hoping that if we won, Wade might get off my back. It was hard not to be happy for Ella, though, who cheered when it was announced. She did a cute, funny little dance in her seat and set us all to laughing.

As we walked back up the mountain, I noticed Alex was hovering nearby. I nudged Ella and told her I was going to go talk to him. She nodded, seeming to understand that we wouldn't want a crowd, and hurried to catch up to Lily, who was walking with her brother.

"Hey," I said as I approached Alex.

He glanced at me and nodded. His face was neutral, but at least it wasn't cold.

"Are you looking forward to the pool party?" I asked.

He shrugged. "I guess."

"I don't swim, so it's kind of a bummer for me."

He looked at me in surprise, and it was the first genuine look I'd seen on his face. "You can't swim?"

I decided to go ahead and lie. There was no way I was getting into a pool, so it wouldn't matter that I did know how—and was rather good at it. No one would ever know. "Nah, not really. I mean, I probably can, I just don't like it."

He looked away and was silent for a few steps. Then he said, "I can't swim, either."

"Hey, no problem. We can hang out together on the side if you want."

That got me a smile, and I was glad to see it. He had a nice smile, and it relaxed his whole face when he did it. "That would be great."

"Okay!"

He didn't say much else after that, but we'd gotten up the mountain by then. I needed to stop in the bathroom, and he went on to the cabin.

The sports bra had been bugging me all morning, and I had to take it off. If I didn't, I was sure a major dysphoria attack would happen. And those usually devolved into panic attacks, which I'd been prone to before I realized I was trans. I didn't want to have a panic attack here, so off came the sports bra. I hated not having my binder on, but my ribs still hurt. The bra hadn't helped them, though it wasn't as bad as the binder.

I put my shirt back on, stuffing my bra into a pocket, and hurried to the cabin for Quiet Time. I actually did sleep that time, since I hadn't gotten much the night before.

Wade had to wake me when the two hours were over. Since we still had a while before dinner, I went out to find Ella so we could hang out.

But I couldn't find her. Instead, I found Gavin reading a book in the Lincoln Lodge. It made me pause, as it was a series I'd made my way through ages ago but loved and would probably read again.

"Is this your first time reading that?" I asked.

He blinked up at me, smiled when he saw it was me, and said, "Yeah. Just found these recently."

"Aren't they great?"

He flipped the book over and examined the cover. It showed a mage fighting a dragon. "Yeah, I guess so. I mean, they're not usually what I read."

"What do you usually like?" I loved fantasy; it was my favorite genre, no matter what people said about it.

"Horror, really. But I'm kinda getting into fantasy because of *Pioneers*."

"Yeah, it will do that."

We chatted for a while, and then he asked, "What's your family like?"

"They're great, actually." I had to be careful here. My family was supportive, for the most part, but I couldn't tell him why. "My mom's nice, but my dad can be annoying sometimes."

"Something we have in common. My dad's a prick."

"Oh, sorry," I said.

"Do you have any siblings?"

"Nah, just me."

"Hunh, I wish. I have three sisters, and I can't stand any of them."

"Sorry." I was unsure what else to say and didn't want to reveal too much about my family, not yet.

The door opened and Alex came in. He looked around, a scowl on his face, and then left. We stared after him, wondering what that was about. Gavin laughed and said, "He's a little strange."

I narrowed my eyes at him. "How so?"

He seemed to sense the difference in attitude and shrugged nonchalantly. "He's...just so quiet."

"Did you hear what Ryan said about him?"

It was Gavin's turn to frown at me. "Yeah, so?"

"Nothing. Just wondering if that's what you thought was weird about him." It came out a little more hostile than I intended.

"Oh! No, that's not what I meant. I mean....no...that's nothing. I mean, it's okay."

I wondered if Gavin would have reacted that way if he was queer. Was he suddenly uncomfortable because he was straight, talking about how it was "okay" to be gay? Or was he worried that I thought he was gay?

"Look," I said, not wanting this to go further. "It's almost time for dinner. I'm going to get changed."

Gavin didn't say anything as I left, and I didn't look back. I was pretty disappointed in him. I selfishly wanted him to be gay or bisexual, but it was more likely he was straight. Statistically speaking, he likely was. Or maybe I wanted to feel that way because I wasn't sure I had a chance with him.

I remembered the moment we had that morning and wondered what he thought about it. Had it made him uncomfortable, and was that why he'd reacted that way? Or had he liked it and didn't know how to deal with it? Had he purposefully tangled himself in the string to get me close and then chickened out? Or had it just been all innocence on his part, and I was reading too much into it? There were so many possibilities, but there was no way I was going to ask him.

Dating while queer was hard. If you outed yourself to someone by asking them out, thinking they might be queer, too, it was always possible they could take offense or even retaliate. They might be homophobic or closeted. And so I always had to be careful. Of course, there were dating apps meant for queer people, but there was no way I was getting on one of those before I was eighteen. I didn't really want to anyway.

It was close to the time for the party, so I headed back to the cabin. Gavin was there, and he ignored me as I came in.

I didn't have a bathing suit with me, but I did have a shirt I didn't mind getting a little wet, should splashing occur. The shirt I was wearing was white, and it would be bad news should it get too wet.

I grabbed the shirt from my trunk and went to the bathroom to change, since the cabin was full of the other boys getting into their swim trunks. I envied them for many reasons, and I tried not to think about any of them as I hastily changed and hurried back.

We went down to dinner as usual, and it was spaghetti and meatballs, which was my absolute favorite dish. Gavin didn't sit with us, and Ella whispered, "What's wrong?" when we had a moment. Lily and Nick were distracted by a heated discussion about something cosplay-related, so for a minute, Ella and I could talk about Gavin.

"I don't know," I said, "but I don't think Gavin is queer."

Ella deflated. "I'm sorry, Casey. That's too bad. Are you sure?"

"No. But...well, it's just the way he acted around Alex, is all."

"Alex?"

"Ryan says he's gay, but I don't know if that's true or not." I sighed. "To be honest, I don't know what to think anymore."

Life at school was so much easier. I knew exactly who was straight, who was gay, who was trans. There were two of us at school—a trans girl and me. Everyone kept trying to get us together, but we didn't have anything in common other than being trans. Still, we were good friends, just as I was with a lot of the other LGTBQ kids. We tended to herd together for protection, even though most of my school was pretty friendly.

We didn't have time to go further with that discussion because Nick and Lily had stopped talking to each other, and we didn't want to risk them listening in on our conversation. I didn't need more people knowing about my crush. Not yet.

After dinner, the counselors told us to go outside and wait, and they would take us to the pool. Apparently it was a different pool than the one we passed every day on the way to meals. They didn't collect us by cabin, which was nice, so I was able to walk with Ella and talk some more. The adults led us through the streets of Ankley Springs, which was quaint in that it looked halfway between a colonial historical town and a Swedish village stuck on the side of a mountain.

"I'm sorry you can't swim with us," Ella said. "I really wish you could just be you here."

"Yeah, I know," I said. "It's okay. There's the whole rest of the summer to swim." We even had a pool in our backyard, so I didn't have to worry about wearing a bathing suit. I could put on a shirt and trunks and not even care about wearing a binder. It was the only swimming I got in these days.

"So, about Alex," Ella said, reminding me. "Have you talked to him?"

"A little. He's quiet and reserved."

"Do you think that's what Gavin might have been talking about?"

"Maybe. I don't know."

"I think you should ask Gavin to the dance."

"Dance? Oh, right." I'd forgotten. There was a dance at the end of the session. "I thought I'd just take you." It wouldn't bring up too many awkward questions.

"Oh, Casey, come on. It's a dance! You can't take me."

"Why not?"

She blew air through her lips, making them flap. "Honestly, how am I ever going to get you married off?"

"Married?" I gasped, playing it up but also secretly horrified at the idea. "Who said anything about marrying anyone?"

She shoved me playfully, and we dissolved into giggles. I was secretly glad she dropped the subject.

The counselors had led us almost to the base of the mountain and an enormous open field bounded by a chain-link fence. But inside was a huge pool, regular sized instead of small like the one near the pavilion. There was also a big stack of wood in the middle of the field, and Ella exclaimed, "Oh, a bonfire!" It hadn't been lit yet, but it would be a big one. "They'll have s'mores!"

I hated marshmallows, but I loved chocolate. Even though, I knew how to roast marshmallows the way Ella liked them, brown all around and as big as a baseball. I had gotten lots of practice at trans camp, after being shown how by one of the counselors there.

Once inside the gates, the other kids ran screaming to the pool. I laughed as Ella joined them, catching the shirt and shorts she tossed away to reveal her rainbow bathing suit.

Following more slowly, I found Alex sitting on one of the deck chairs off to one side and asked, "Is this seat taken?"

He shook his head without looking at me. I sat down and folded up Ella's clothing to put under the chair, hopefully far enough away from the water it wouldn't get wet.

"Is she your girlfriend?" Alex asked, to my surprise.

"Nah," I said. "She's just a good friend."

"Really? You're so close I thought you were dating. How long have you known her?"

"Nah, we've been friends forever. Almost my whole life."

I wanted to ask him about his friends, but I didn't want to ask him if he had any at all. That sounded weird, like I didn't believe he did. But I hadn't seen him be social with anyone at all. I could see him struggling to keep his face impassive, and I wondered what he was hiding.

"I wish I had someone like that," he said, answering my question.

"I'm sorry. I know it's kind of rare." Was he interested in Ella?

"My parents move a lot. I'm usually never in the same place more than a couple of years."

"Army?"

"No." he said, shaking his head. "My dad's an engineer. He works with the Navy, though, so we move when they need us to." He curled up and put his head on his knees, his arms wrapped around them. It was a precarious way to sit on a deck chair, but he managed it.

"So what do you like to do?" I asked, not wanting to talk much about family.

"Why are you asking me?"

"Oh." I looked away, trying not to be offended. Maybe there was someone else I could talk to? I was about to get up to look around, but he put a hand out to stop me.

"Sorry," he interrupted, before I could say anything else. "Just...not used to people being interested in me."

"Why not?"

"I'm always the new guy, right? No one likes the new guy."

"That's not always true."

"Says the dude who's had a friend all his life."

I couldn't refute that, so I didn't say anything. We watched the kids splashing in the water.

"Look," Alex said after a few minutes of awkward silence. "It's been nice. Thanks for talking with me." He stood up and left the pool area to go to the pile of wood. It still hadn't been lit, but it wasn't dark yet.

I watched him go, a little disappointed. He was right. I didn't know what it was like to be the new guy, not like that. But I did know what it was like to switch schools. Ella had done the same thing, though, following me to the new school so we could be together. It was true: I had always had a good friend, no matter what.

I turned to see what Ella was doing. She was paddling up and down the pool lazily, with Lily following. Ella was very carefully not getting her hair wet—she had coiled it up on her head with a clip—and she eyed the boys who were horsing around with disdain as they splashed water her way.

The urge to jump in and join my friends was strong, but that would be a disaster. A wet shirt would cling to every curve, revealing my secret.

The splashing increased until I got a little damp. Not wanting to risk getting too wet, I went to the side of the pool to tell Ella where her clothes were, so I could go hang out by the not-yet-lit bonfire.

I didn't see Ryan.

I leaned over the water to shout at Ella, who was on the other side of the pool. She glanced in my direction, and her expression was my only warning.

Ryan burst out of the water right in front of me, slinging an armload of water right up into my face. Out of sheer surprise, I inhaled, right as the water hit me. Some of it went down my lungs, the chlorine burning my throat. Coughing and choking, my throat spasmed closed. I was trying desperately to simultaneously clear my lungs and suck air down. I couldn't tell what was going on, but I was starting to panic. My world narrowed down to the ache in my lungs and my lack of air.

I lost my balance and fell straight into the pool.

Instinctively, I curled around my chest, hiding my breasts with my arms. Panic gripped me, and I couldn't breathe. *I couldn't breathe.*

Hands grabbed at me, and in my terror, I slapped them away. I was still trying to inhale and cough at the same time, and dark spots were starting to appear in my vision.

But I finally managed to stand—the water wasn't deep—and expelled the water from my lungs. I sucked in a shaky breath, but the panic had gripped me. The breath wasn't enough.

I started to hyperventilate instead, overcompensating.

More hands grabbed at me, but I smacked them away, splashing and kicking until my head bumped the side of the pool. The pain wasn't bad, but it sent my already panicking brain into overdrive, and I flailed and slipped under the water again.

I didn't remember much beyond that, other than finally being dragged out of the pool. My head was in Ella's lap, and the panic was slowly receding. When my vision cleared, I realized I had gone temporarily blind, literally blind with panic.

"There you are," said Ella, smiling down at me. It was more a worried grimace than a grin, and her eyes were red.

"Sorry," I choked out. My throat was raw.

She patted my cheek. "Shh, no, don't apologize."

"That was a bad one." It felt like I'd tried to swallow an entire pineapple.

"Yeah, but don't worry about it."

"They know, don't they?"

"Know what?"

I just looked at her meaningfully. She shook her head. She tugged on something, and I dimly realized she had wrapped a towel around me. It was rough on my skin, but it was warm.

I could have kissed her. "Are you sure?"

"No, but I think they got you out of the pool fast enough. I was right there with the towel."

She looked away and nodded, her mouth moving, and I realized she was responding to someone else. I had tuned out everything around me. As far as I was concerned, Ella and I were the only people who existed in the world. My brain hadn't been able to handle anything else.

I turned my head and saw Wade's worried face. "How are you doing?" He sounded like he was at the bottom of a well, his voice distorted and strange as my brain tried to sort out all the stimuli.

"Okay now," I said.

"We called an ambulance. Do you want to go with them?"

"Oh, shit," I blurted, but he didn't chastise me for it. "No, no, I'm fine." I sat up and actually did feel fine.

Wade eyed me critically, like he didn't believe me. "Are you sure? We called your parents, and they said it's up to you. They want to talk to you, though."

"I'm fine, really. Can I just go sit by the fire?" I hadn't planned on getting wet, and now that I had, I could feel the cool mountain air more than before. My fingers were numb, but that might still be from the panic, too. I started to shiver.

Wade and Ella helped me up. I tried not to notice everyone staring at me. The pool had gone quiet, and none of the kids were in it anymore. They must have evacuated it to make sure everyone else was safe.

They guided me to the pile of wood, which still hadn't been lit. Ella sat down next to me, her arm wrapped protectively around me, and Wade produced a lighter. He bent over the wood, and within a few minutes, the fire was burning brightly.

I wiped at my face with the towel, clutching it with nerveless fingers. For the moment, it was all that kept me from being discovered as being trans.

The fire wasn't producing much heat yet, but it felt good on my face. I leaned into Ella. "Thank you. I love you."

"I love you, too. I'm so sorry, Casey. I didn't see him in time. Damn him!"

"Let's not talk about that now." My throat almost closed over the words. I couldn't afford to panic again, not so soon after. I didn't want to think about how I had almost drowned, and how it was Ryan's fault.

"Okay."

We sat in silence for a long time, while I watched the flames consume the wood. Ella held on to me tightly, fending off anyone who wanted to come up and talk. There were many reasons I loved her, and this was one of them. She knew exactly what I needed, when I needed it.

I would do the same for her.

Other kids had joined the circle around the fire, but I tuned them out, too. When I felt stronger, I was able to look around. They were laughing and having fun, as though they hadn't just seen me freak out. That was good.

I hadn't had a panic attack like that in a long time. It had probably been brought on by not being able to wear my binder all day and having to wear that stupid bra instead. And the fear I'd already had about getting wet. Body dysphoria and a sudden fright were not good for my mental health.

"What happened to Ryan?" I asked suddenly, ready now to know the answer.

"His dad came to get him."

"Good."

Ella paused and then carefully said, "I don't think they'll make him leave camp permanently, though. He was arguing with his dad over it when they left."

I frowned. I didn't want to be in the same cabin as Ryan anymore. Maybe I could ask to move to another one, or maybe they'd make him move.

I sat up away from Ella, and she let me. She handed me some chocolate and said, "I know you don't like s'mores, but here's some candy."

I devoured the candy bar in seconds. Wade was handing out metal pokers, marshmallows, and more candy. "I'll roast one for you," I told Ella.

"You don't have to."

"I want to."

She handed me a poker and a marshmallow she'd gotten from Wade. I stuck the marshmallow on, edgewise rather than through the end, and stuck it into the flames. Roasting a marshmallow properly was an exercise in patience. You had to rotate it just right, browning it evenly on all sides. You had to watch the flames, so they wouldn't light the marshmallow on fire. It was therapeutic, because it made me think of something other than the close call I'd had.

After several moments, it was ready—evenly brown all over, still sizzling from the heat, and so large you couldn't eat it in one bite. I pulled it out of the fire and quickly handed the poker to Ella. Her eyes were shining as she bit into the marshmallow. She melted a little, too, making muffled appreciative noises.

"You are so awesome," she said with her mouth still full of molten sugar.

We sat there in companionable silence for a while, leaning against one another, until I heard footsteps approaching and turned to see who it was. Ella looked as though she was about to shoo him away, but I stopped her. It was Gavin.

"Is it okay if I sit?" he asked.

"Sure," I said, and Ella looked at me meaningfully. I knew what she was asking, and I shook my head, wanting her to stay. She settled down and leaned hard into me as though daring Gavin to ask her to leave.

Gavin sat down, but on the opposite side of Ella from me. "Are you okay?" he asked, sounding genuinely concerned.

"I'm getting there."

"I'm sorry Ryan is such a dick."

That startled a laugh out of me. "Not your fault." The laugh made my throat hurt, but it felt good to laugh.

"What he did was really bad."

"Yeah, it was."

"So...um..." He looked uncomfortable and then scratched at his head. His face was lit by the flames, his freckles nearly gone in the half-light. "So...I, uh, don't know how to say this..." He looked helpless.

"Ella, could you give us a minute?"

She hesitated and then squeezed my shoulder as she stood up and wandered off. But I could see her watching us, motherly in her protection of me.

"What is it?"

"I...uh...I saw you. When you were underwater."

"What?"

"You. Your...chest..."

Oh. Shit. "Dammit." I'd hoped he wanted to talk to me about something else. Now I wished I hadn't asked Ella to leave.

"So, you're like a girl or something?"

I turned my frozen gaze on him. "No. I am not a girl." Anger had replaced fear. "I am a boy. I'm trans." I said it quietly, even though I wanted to shout it at him, and the cowardice made me hate myself a little. So what? I was trans. I should scream it from the rooftops as something to be proud of. I shouldn't hide it. But because everyone else hated us, I had to conceal the part of me I loved the most.

"Oh. Okay."

"Okay?" His response threw me. I expected revulsion, confusion, condemnation, but not this. "You mean, you're okay with it?" I said it before I could stop myself, and I could feel the embarrassment painting my cheeks red.

He put his chin on his hands, leaning forward with his elbows on his knees, and looked at me. His eyes were sparkling in the firelight. "I guess. I mean...whatever, right?"

"What's that supposed to mean?"

"I don't think it makes any difference."

"Difference?"

"To me."

"Thanks. I think."

"No...I mean..."

My heart suddenly lurched in my chest. He had scooted even closer to me. His face was too close. His eyelids had lowered, that bright fringe of red falling onto his pale cheeks. Panic was rising again, and I desperately tried to swallow it back down, not wanting another attack. I tried to tell my overextended nervous system this was a good thing. It wasn't listening.

I reeled to my feet. I couldn't do this. Not right now.

The world spun around me, and my fingers tingled.

Hating myself a little, I ran away from Gavin. He was calling after me, but I couldn't stop—couldn't turn around and go back. When I returned to the poolside, I grabbed Ella's clothes from under the chair. I found her nearby and shoved them at her.

"I want to go back to the cabin."

"Oh, okay." She accepted her clothes and pulled them back on.

We went together to find Wade. The pool party wasn't over, but I knew they'd make an exception for me. He did agree to take us back on the condition we stop at the nurse's station and talk to my parents. I was okay with that, so he walked with us up the mountain.

I was quiet the whole time, but Ella and Wade talked as we went. I didn't listen to them since I had to concentrate on not panicking and on quelling the self-hatred slowly rising inside me. I clutched the towel to me, a flimsy protection against my feelings and the imagined stares of the campers and the townspeople.

Everything I wanted had been handed to me on a platter. Gavin knew I was trans, and he didn't care. He'd been leaning in to kiss me; I was sure. A cute boy who knew I was trans liked me and wanted to kiss me.

And instead of enjoying it, I had nearly panicked again. *Damn it.*

All the way to the nurse's house, I tried to convince myself I didn't really want to kiss Gavin. I'd repeatedly said, out loud and to myself, that I hadn't come for romance. Heck, I hadn't even looked at most of the girls. That thought made me even more angry, because clearly one part of me *had* come for the romance. But I didn't want that to be the part of me that was in control. I wanted to have fun and be just like all the other boys.

The nurse was happy to let us in, and led me to the ancient phone, cord and all, stuck on the wall of her kitchen.

I both did and didn't want to talk to my parents but knew they'd be worried. I wouldn't admit it to myself, but I needed to hear my mom's voice. The past couple of days had been hard.

The phone rang but was picked up almost immediately.

"Hello?"

"Hi Mom, it's me."

"Oh my god, Casey. Are you okay? What happened? Who did this?"

"Mom…"

"Do you want us to come get you? We can come tonight and be there in less than two hours."

"Mom!" I finally had to shout, and Wade frowned at me. "I'm fine. No, you don't need to come up. I'm okay."

"Are you sure? Your dad and I are worried about you."

"It's okay, really. Please, don't worry. I'm fine. It was just a panic attack. I didn't wear my binder today, and then I slipped into the pool. I'm okay."

"Your counselor said another kid tried to hurt you." Her voice was so hard—she knew I was trying to hide things from her.

"It was just a prank. He splashed me and surprised me, and I fell in. I'm fine."

"Your dad wants to speak to you."

"No…" I didn't want to talk to him. I wasn't sure I could take the disappointment in his voice. But she wasn't listening and had handed the phone over to him anyway.

"Are you okay, Casey?" he blurted out.

I paused. My dad rarely used my name. I knew it was because he missed my old name, my deadname. He'd picked it out when I was born. I picked out Casey. "Yeah, Dad, I'm fine," was all I could choke out.

"Are you sure? You don't want to come home?"

"No, it's okay." I could feel the word I wanted to hear hovering between us. He'd called me by my name, but could he call me...son?

He sounded gruff. "Well, that's good then. I'm sorry you're having a hard time there, Casey."

My heart leaped in my chest again. "Thanks Dad. I...I love you, Dad."

"I love you too...Casey."

Tears welled up in my eyes. I hadn't ever heard him say that before, to that name. I heard the hesitation, but he'd said it. I sniffled, but no one heard, because he'd handed the phone back to my mom.

"Casey, you just call us again if you want to come home, okay? You don't have to put up with bullying, you know. Call us right away if anything else happens. We'll be there for you."

"Hey Mom...have you been talking with Dad?" I had to know.

"About what?"

"About...you know, my transition?"

"Well, yes, but not recently. You...you know what he's like."

Yeah, I knew what it was like. He'd walk away, or not say anything but sit there, stone-faced and disapproving. But...if she hadn't been saying anything... "He...he called me by my name."

"I know. I know it's been hard, Casey. Just be patient with him, okay?"

"Sure." I could be patient with him, but would he ever come around?

"He's worried about you, you know," she said, almost whispering it.

Something in my chest gave way, and I had to swallow hard so I wouldn't start crying again. "Thanks, Mom," I said, meaning it.

We said goodbye and then hung up. I felt a little better for having talked with them. Especially my dad. He was worried about me. He cared about me, enough to call me by my name after all of this.

Wade took us up to the cabins, and there was an awkward moment of trying to figure out what to do with us. He finally relented and allowed Ella to come into our cabin. He certainly couldn't allow her to be alone, and none of the other counselors had come with us.

"But I'm not leaving," he warned us, unnecessarily.

That was fine. I wasn't sure I wanted to be alone anyway, in case I had another panic attack, even though I was fairly sure I wasn't going to. At least, not right now, not after talking with my parents. Ella had helped me through them before, but it was usually better if an adult was around in case I accidentally hurt myself.

Ella and I got onto my bed, and we sat as close to each other as Wade would allow. Wade settled himself into his own bunk and ignored us as we talked quietly.

"I'm so sorry this happened," Ella said.

"It's okay. Don't worry about it."

"But what about Gavin?" she said, mouthing his name, and looked at Wade. At that point, I didn't care who knew what. Since Wade knew I was trans, he might as well know I was bisexual, too.

I shrugged. "It's probably better this way."

"Why? What do you mean?"

"It's too complicated. I came here to just have fun." I could now see the lie. I ignored it and convinced myself it was the truth.

Ella frowned at me, as though she knew what I was thinking and feeling. And maybe she did. She knew me as well as I knew myself, perhaps better. But she didn't say anything, respecting my wish to continue with the self-delusion.

We talked about other things, lighter things, until it was nearing bedtime. Wade hustled Ella to leave the cabin as soon as the other kids started coming back up the mountain, and she hugged me good night.

To my relief, Ryan did not return. Neither Alex nor Gavin would look at me, and I couldn't blame them. No one else talked to me, either, clearly uncomfortable with my public panic attack. Ryan's friends, Geoff, Tyler, and Tanner, threw me black looks as though it was all my fault. Nick was the only one who spoke to me.

"You doing okay, man?" he asked.

"Yeah, fine." I thanked him and tried not to be bitter that he was the only one who cared enough to ask.

Wade let me go shower, which I hurriedly did as there was very little hot water. Shivering, I ran back to the cabin and got into bed.

I lay there awake again, staring at the ceiling, and then out the mesh window. I'd gone through the whole gamut of emotions that night. I wanted to go home. I wanted to stay. I wanted to come out to everyone and get it over with. I wanted to stay in the closet and never come out to anyone ever again. I was happy Ryan was gone. I was upset he would likely return. I wished Gavin had kissed me. I wished I'd never met Gavin. I hated myself for having a crush. I loved crushing on Gavin, who was adorable. It made me feel wonderful that he obviously liked me. But then it made me feel horrible he knew I was trans, even though he'd said it was fine.

Sometime in the night, exhaustion from the roller coaster of emotions finally overtook me, and I slept.

Chapter Four

I WOKE UP, still tired, before everyone else. My sleep had been deep, but I hadn't had enough of it. However, I felt better than I had in a while. That sometimes happened after panic attacks. It was as though my body had been purged of all the negative emotions and was left lighter, happier. It never lasted, but at least I got to enjoy it while it did.

After gathering up my clothes—including my binder—I rushed out to the bathroom to get dressed. It was a huge relief to finally wear it again. My chest was back to being as flat as I wished it would be all the time.

When I returned, Ryan was back. He was laughing it up with his friends in the cabin, and they all ignored me when I came back in. That was just as well. I think my heart stopped for a moment when I opened the door and saw him there. It had caught me off guard. I'd hoped he'd be gone longer than one night, or, even better, for the rest of the session.

To my surprise, though, Gavin smiled at me when I came back in and asked, "Did you sleep well?"

"No, not really." His attention had surprised me enough I hadn't thought to lie.

It wasn't the answer he was clearly expecting, and he just said, "Oh, sorry."

While everyone else was getting dressed, I started making my bed. I also had cleaning duties with another cabin, and it was the latrines again. Wonderful. I kicked rocks back into place around the entrance to my cabin and then went to the latrines to do the showers.

When we lined up to go eat breakfast, Gavin was right there. "So what sorts of activities do you think they'll have today?" he asked.

I stared at him for a moment, trying to decide whether he was being nice to me just because or whether he was playing with me. "Don't know. But I'm kind of hoping it will be something different. I don't want to do friendship bracelets or dodgeball again."

"Yeah, same here."

Even more surprising, Alex came up to us and joined in the conversation. "Anyone know what we're having for breakfast?"

Gavin and I both stared at him long enough that he started to turn away, anger written clearly on his face. I stopped him by catching his arm. "Sorry, yeah, don't know. Whatever it is, it'll probably be good."

He looked at my hand on his arm and then up at me. A tiny smile tugged at the corner of his mouth.

It was a little awkward and stilted, but we made small talk on the way down the mountain. It was kind of like we were getting to know one another again—a fresh start. I learned that Alex lived with his dad, that his mother had died when he was still really young. Gavin's parents were still together, but he'd said his dad was a prick. We commiserated a bit about overprotective parents.

They both asked to sit with us at breakfast. I'd never seen Alex hanging out with other people, though admittedly I hadn't been paying attention. That made me feel bad.

Ella made eyes at me when Gavin sat down right next to me, and I just smiled and threw one shoulder up into a "we'll see what happens" sort of shrug. She tried containing her excitement for me, though she didn't hide it well. She was practically vibrating in her chair and was extra loud when she spoke to anyone.

I did feel better about possibly getting involved with Gavin. He was a nice guy, at least as far as I could tell. I still wasn't sure I wanted to get into a romance at camp, though. What could we do? Sneak off to kiss? We certainly couldn't be out in the open with it. I couldn't ask him to the dance, could I?

While the world had become more accepting of same-sex romances, I wasn't sure a camp full of kids I didn't know would be the best place to test it out. At least, not without a few adults that I knew I could trust running things. Wade might be useful, but since Ryan's uncle owned the place, I wasn't willing to try it out.

I remembered Ella had said there were a lot of queer people here, and that might be true. But I hadn't really seen any. There were no gay couples smooching in the open. Maybe that would change by the time we all started thinking about dates for the dance, or maybe it wouldn't. I still wasn't sure I wanted to find out firsthand how queer-friendly this camp was or wasn't.

Breakfast was biscuits and gravy with home fries. It was so good I stuffed myself silly as I chatted with Ella, Nick, Lily, Alex, and Gavin.

Alex was quiet most of the time, but he was starting to come out of his shell. Lily and Nick took the addition of the two boys in stride. Gavin and Nick were fans of a video game I hadn't played before, and they geeked out over it for several minutes.

Lily, Ella, and I got into a discussion of cosplay again, and I listened, fascinated, as Lily described a new build she was working on. It sounded insanely complex, but I could tell she enjoyed doing it and the attention it was getting her.

Because I tended to like boys a little more than girls, I hadn't ever noticed Lily that much. But now I realized how pretty she was. Taking a girl to the dance would be infinitely easier than trying to take a boy.

But Lily didn't make my heart flutter the way Gavin did.

Besides, I'd already said I'd go with Ella unless some miracle happened and I could take Gavin without causing a huge fuss. Ella certainly wasn't going to ask anyone, and I didn't want her to feel left out.

After breakfast, we all walked together back up the mountain to sign up for our morning activities. There were the usual dodgeball and ultimate Frisbee options. Instead of bracelet making, there was a nature hike, which sounded nice. Ella, Gavin, Alex, and I all signed up for the hike.

We were to meet at cabin twelve, which was further down the road than I'd gone before. Boys generally weren't allowed down that end since it was where all the girls' cabins were, and it felt a little rebellious as we passed by them.

Lars was the counselor for the hike, and he was joined by one of the women counselors, Angela, who was in charge of cabin eleven. She was a black woman with medium brown skin and an array of tight black braids she'd pulled up into a huge bun on top of her head. Lars actually wore sensible hiking clothes that morning, though his pants had been poorly tie-dyed. He stared at nothing as we all gathered, humming to himself.

We waited for a while, making sure everyone who wanted to come had a chance to sign up. Angela went back to the lodge and checked to make sure the list had been filled up and then called our names out so she'd know who we all were.

"Okay!" she said. "Let's get going!"

We even went past cabin number thirteen, which I hadn't known was there, and the road still kept going up the mountain. I wondered where it went, and if we were going to be following it.

Lars began pointing out interesting plants as we passed. I wasn't interested in trees, but I dutifully listened as we went. The road petered out into a trail at a stand of maples. Lars listed all the different kinds of trees we were seeing, but I couldn't tell them apart.

I was too distracted by Gavin. He'd changed into a tank top and shorts. It wasn't entirely smart when tromping through the woods, but it showed off his arms and strong legs. I envied his flat chest and how he was able to wear a tank top effortlessly, without needing a binder.

I was sweating into my binder, and my breathing was too shallow. Though we'd only just started walking uphill, my T-shirt had started to cling to me. The day was heating up, and I was already miserable.

Ella was casting worried glances at me, but I waved her on. Gavin looked back at me but continued with the others. I slowed a bit to catch my breath and then hurried to get back with the group, hating that they might think I was out of shape or something. I told myself I was fine, that I shouldn't start worrying. It might set off a dysphoria attack, which wouldn't help anything right now.

Angela and Lars had stopped pointing out plants, as they'd run out of ones to list, and instead, chatted with each other. That left the rest of us to our own devices, as long as we followed them.

We continued along the trail, which turned rougher as we went up the mountain. Now, it was a thin strip between the trees—barely a string of rocks along the barren ground that we stepped over or stumbled on. A few times, it got steep enough where I had to use my hands for balance. I wondered how long we'd be hiking, and if we'd miss lunch if we went too far.

I stumbled once, and Gavin caught my hand as it waved frantically. A thrill went up my arm, and again when he didn't let go.

He smiled shyly back at me as we held hands. I was blushing, and so was he. His face was bright enough to match his hair, his freckles drowning in a tide of red. Even his ears were crimson.

Gavin's hand was warm in mine, but I was pretty sure mine was sweaty and dirty from when I'd fallen. I hoped he didn't care. I was struggling through a mountain climb with a binder on, and he was wearing a tank top and shorts. I was going to be hot.

We tried to make it casual. I was hoping no one would notice, but eventually he ended up helping me out a few places, and it felt like everyone took note of how much hand-holding we were doing. Ella translated her excitement for me into bounding from rock to rock as they got big enough to stand on the higher we went.

After about an hour of walking, Lars and Angela called a halt. We were close to where they wanted to take us, but they weren't sure we'd get there in time. We still had to make it all the way back, though we had plenty of time before lunch.

"Down will be easier," Lars said when Angela showed doubt as to whether we could make it. "It'll go faster."

"Okay, let's try it then," Angela said.

The rest was brief, but it gave Gavin and me a chance to sit together. His knee was touching mine, and I was acutely aware of it. I couldn't believe this was actually happening to me. And we were doing it out in the open. All of the other kids could clearly see us holding hands and sitting close.

My heart wouldn't stop doing flip-flops in my chest, and I felt a little nauseated. I couldn't believe I was sitting there, in the open, with Gavin. Who knew I was trans. Who didn't care that I was trans.

I had to be dreaming.

I pinched myself a few times just to make sure, but I didn't wake up.

I didn't pay much attention to the rest of the nature walk, because I was too busy paying attention to Gavin. We didn't talk much, only held hands and walked. And looked at each other. And at the ground, too embarrassed to make eye contact again. I tried to think of funny or clever things to say, but they all sounded so ridiculous they never made it to my lips. Probably a good thing. I didn't want to scare Gavin away by being too weird.

But when we arrived where Lars and Angela had been leading us, it was worth the whole hike. I paid attention then.

We came out of the trees onto a nearly flat expanse of bare rock, and suddenly there was a valley stretched out below us. Mist had collected in the bowl of the valley, but it was slowly dissipating in the sunlight. We were so high up the trees below us looked like a carpet of green, stretching out as far as I could see. It seemed as though the whole world was green forest. A hawk called out above us, soaring on the wind.

"Wow," I whispered.

Gavin and I found a place on the rock to sit, but it was precarious. I felt like I could easily slide down the rock and out into the air, falling forever to the valley below. I'd never been up so high, and I didn't like it. But Gavin was there, and he was holding my hand. I gulped and tried not to think about falling.

"We're so high up." My voice was shaking. I hadn't realized I was so scared of heights. I did want to go closer to the edge but didn't think my brain would let me.

Gavin pushed himself closer to me. "It's okay; I have you."

And before I could stop him, he wrapped his arms around me, pulling me as close to him as I could get. I was practically on his lap, could feel his breath at my ear.

"Is this better?" he asked.

"Yes," I whispered, unable to say anything more loudly.

"Is this okay?"

"Yes." Still unable to say anything more than just that one word.

"Why did you run away?" he asked quietly.

"I'm sorry. I...I was just not ready. Not right then."

"Are you ready now?"

I turned in his arms to look into his eyes. "Ready for what?"

A grin spread over his face, and he must have known what I was thinking. "Dating," was what he said, though.

My heart tripped in my chest. "Dating?"

"Yeah, you know...us going out?"

I didn't know what to tell him. Was I ready to date? Like, really date? Or could we just stay like this forever?

I never got a chance to answer, because a commotion broke out behind us.

"Where's Alex?" Lars' voice was tense, alerting us all that something was very wrong.

I snapped out of my haze of joy and looked around. Alex wasn't there. I thought I'd just seen him, and he definitely had started out with us.

With a wash of shame, I realized I hadn't even paid attention to anyone other than Gavin over the past hour.

Ella hadn't minded (she'd been making googly eyes at us the whole time), but had Alex felt left out? Or had he gotten lost?

Lars fell right out of his dreamy-hippie personality and went straight back down the path with purpose, calling Alex's name.

Angela stayed with us, but she searched the woods within sight of us to see if maybe he'd gone off to answer nature's call without telling anyone.

"What do you think happened?" Ella asked as we gathered together back on the path. She'd started chewing on her nails.

"He probably just went to the bathroom," Gavin said.

"Yeah." I wanted it to be true, too. It would be awful if he'd gotten lost.

"Did you see him leave?" Ella looked at us. I shook my head, and Gavin did, too.

"I feel bad," I said. "He'd come with us."

"He probably went into the woods," Gavin said, and I tried to convince myself that was what had happened.

But Angela returned without having found him. "We'll wait here for a while, to see if he comes back," she said.

We stayed there longer than we should have, but Lars returned and shook his head. "Can't find him," he said. "We need to go back and let everyone know."

Too bad cell phones wouldn't work up here.

Gavin and I didn't hold hands on the way down. It was impossible, anyway, since we had to jump from rock to rock in some places.

The walk back did take less time than the walk up, but by the time we got back, Lars and Angela were in a near panic. We still hadn't seen any sign of Alex. I felt guilty, and I could tell from the expression on their faces that Gavin and Ella did, too. We'd gotten too wrapped up in ourselves to notice what had happened to our new friend.

Once the cabins were in sight, Lars took me and Gavin straight to our cabin while Angela made sure everyone else got back to theirs safely. Lars barged right on in and looked around. Alex wasn't there, but Wade was.

Our counselor rolled off of his bed when he saw Lars and said, "What's up, man?"

"Have you seen Alex?"

"Not recently."

Lars swore under his breath. "He was on the nature walk with us and then disappeared."

We were given firm orders to stay there while Wade and Lars both rushed out of the cabin.

Gavin and I were alone.

Had it been under other circumstances, it would have been great. Fantastic, even, being alone with a boy with no supervision. But I worried for Alex.

"What do you think happened?" I echoed Ella's question from earlier.

"No idea." Gavin seemed uninterested. Instead, he took my arm and sat me down on his bed. I immediately started to shake. I was sitting on his bed. Alone. "So, do you like me or not?"

I was stunned by the sudden question, the abrupt change of subject. I stammered out, "Uh, yeah, I guess so."

"Guess so?"

"Just...you know..." I looked away, unable to answer the question. It was too embarrassing.

He touched my cheek with a finger and ran it down my jaw. "Soft."

I laughed a little too bitterly. "Can't start testosterone yet." It was out before I could stop it. Normally, I didn't like discussing my transition with most people.

"Oh, wow. So...you really are trans."

I looked back at him. "Yeah." I wondered what he meant.

"Sorry, I haven't ever met anyone who was. I mean, like, really met them."

"Does it bother you?"

"No."

He would never know the relief that flooded my body when he said that one word. His finger trailed to my bottom lip, brushing it lightly. I closed my eyes and tried not to faint. I could feel all the blood in my body, rushing through my veins, and I was aware of all of my skin. My binder was tight and itchy.

"I never thought I'd, you know. Be attracted to someone who was."

I opened my eyes again and stared at him, letting him see the offense on my face. "Why? Because we're freaks?"

He snatched his hand back. "No. That's not what I meant. Just...I don't know." He slumped and looked away guiltily. "Maybe."

Disappointment replaced the relief. But I wasn't surprised. "I know. You've only seen us on TV or in tabloids. We're not all like that. We're real people. I'm lucky. I came out at a young age. I won't go through full puberty until I'm ready, until I'm sure I want to be a man."

"Are you sure?"

"Yes. But they're still going to make me wait. My parents and my doctors. I might be able to go on testosterone at sixteen if my parents agree to it. But they won't."

"I thought you said they were cool."

"Yeah, mostly. My dad is resisting. He's coming around, but I think he'll make me wait until I'm eighteen." I still wasn't sure why I was telling him this. He didn't need to know it, but for some reason, I wanted him to.

"That's terrible."

"Yeah."

I'd also have to wait even longer for top surgery—for getting my chest flattened. Most doctors wouldn't even discuss it until after a year of being on hormones, and I had to turn eighteen before they'd consider permanent changes anyway. That meant, at the earliest, I could have my surgery at nineteen, and it seemed like such a long time from now. It felt unattainable. Five more years of crushing my ribs with a binder. Five more years of not being as physically active as I wanted to be—namely in swimming—because I couldn't be on a boys' team if I had breasts. And even if they let me...what would be the point? I couldn't compete with boys my age, not now anyway. Maybe if I'd been training harder, started earlier. But without testosterone, I didn't have the upper body power. I could still do it, if I found a team willing to take me, but it would be such an uphill battle I wasn't sure it would be worth it.

I suppose Gavin didn't have anything else to say to that, which was probably a good thing. Because Ryan came in then, banging the door open so hard it made us both jump. We scooted away from each other a little guiltily.

Ryan caught the movement. He sneered at us. "Just what are you queers doing?"

"Go away," said Gavin.

Ryan raised an eyebrow. "Oh? You're going to talk to me like that? After what I told you before? Did you forget?"

Gavin stiffened but didn't say anything.

Ryan was staring him down, and Gavin was the first to look away. "That's what I thought." Ryan turned his back and got into his bunk, chuckling maliciously to himself.

I didn't know what was going on, or what Ryan meant, but Gavin had pulled away, withdrawing into himself. He wouldn't look at me. I took the hint, got up, and climbed into my own bed. It felt cowardly, slinking away back to my own bunk, leaving Gavin alone below. But I was acutely aware of every move he made.

There was nothing to do but wait. Lunch had been postponed until Alex could be found, and everyone was rushing around getting to their cabins. With great relief, though, Wade came in only a few minutes later with a chastened-looking Alex in tow. I sat up in my bed, hopped off, and nearly jumped the two steps to get to Alex.

"You're okay!" I said, maybe a bit too enthusiastically.

He looked at me and said nothing. He just stood there and stared at me.

"Alex?"

Wade was watching us and then said, "Alex just returned to camp on his own. He's been here the whole time."

"Leave me alone," Alex said before I could get a word out. He pushed past me and went to his bed.

I didn't even have time to think about it before Wade hustled us out for lunch. Alex never looked at us. Gavin and I stood together, but didn't touch, as we waited for everyone to line up.

Why had Alex left? Was it because of Gavin and me?

He...he couldn't like Gavin, could he? Or me? I didn't want to think it was me, because having two guys like me at the same time was a situation that was too bizarre to be real. Of course, it would be fantastic, but I was sure he liked Gavin, not me.

Alex didn't sit with us at lunch, but no one else seemed to notice anything was amiss. Only Gavin and I kept glancing at him once in a while. Maybe it was in hopes that he'd be looking at us, maybe so we could show him we still wanted to be friends.

Ella's cabin once again got the Clean Cabin Award, disappointing Gavin and me. We'd been working so hard!

Alex continued to ignore us as we finished up the meal.

After lunch, we went to sign up for our activities. There were the usual ones, but a new one caught my eye. There was space for only six people. On the paper, the actual activity name wasn't listed. Instead were the words, "Something Special. Bring a mattress."

Nothing else appealed, but what could we possibly need a mattress for? The possibilities didn't seem innocent to me, but maybe that was a failure of imagination.

I signed up for it, and so did Gavin and Ella.

We separated for Quiet Time. Alex ignored us still as we came in, turning his back as I came near. I wanted to talk to him, but he clearly didn't want to talk. So I left him alone, but I felt so bad inside. What had I done? I tried not to feel guilty for being chosen by Gavin. I couldn't be ashamed of that, could I? But I was, strangely.

I didn't sleep that hour, but instead lay staring at the ceiling and worrying. Had we done something to offend Alex? Had we hurt his feelings? Could he really like one of us and was now jealous or angry that we seemed to be together? Had anyone else done anything to him?

Maybe Wade knew? He saw Alex when he came back, heard him say to stay away from him. Maybe he knew why?

It made me feel terrible that I had potentially said or done something to offend him. I tried my best to get along with everyone, though I knew I failed often.

There wasn't anything I could do about it right then. I'd have to see if I could try to get Alex to talk later.

When Quiet Time was over, Gavin and I dragged our mattresses off of our beds and pulled them into Lincoln Lodge.

To no one's surprise, it was Lars who was presiding over the unusual and mysterious activity. Ella arrived soon after with her own mattress, and Lars directed us to arrange them in lines. Three other campers came in and joined us, their faces showing their curiosity.

I was in the middle, between Ella and Gavin. Lars directed us to move our mattresses farther apart, which we did, though reluctantly. I think we all wanted to be close together for whatever he had planned.

"Okay," he said, his voice soft and his eyes staring off into the distance. Was he on something or was it just the way he was? He'd snapped out of it quickly, though, when he'd thought Alex was lost. It was probably the way he was. "Today, we're going to learn some interesting meditation techniques."

Well, that was disappointing. Meditation? Why would I want to learn that?

"Everyone get on your mattresses and lie down," he commanded, and we complied. Gavin and I shared exasperated looks.

"Now close your eyes and relax."

I did, but I wasn't sure I was going to be able to relax. This was so ridiculous.

"Feel yourself sinking into the mattress. You've gotten very heavy."

His voice had started in a drone, and it was more annoying than relaxing.

"Sink deep into your mattress. Imagine yourself actually sinking down into the ground below—you've gotten so heavy."

I had to bite my lip to keep from giggling. This was so silly, and I felt ridiculous there, spread out over my bare mattress on the floor of Lincoln Lodge.

I startled when I felt fingers on my hand. Gavin had scooted as far as he could to one side of his mattress so he could reach out and just barely touch my arm. When I smiled at him, he grinned back and winked.

I reached out to him, and our fingers wove together. It didn't seem so silly now.

He closed his eyes and so did I, but I couldn't concentrate on what Lars was saying. I was too aware of the warm hand in mine, the thrill that ran through me every time I realized he liked me.

At some point, he squeezed my hand, and I opened my eyes to look at him. He mouthed something at me, but I couldn't read his lips. I shook my head and looked at him quizzically. He waved a hand and looked away again.

Lars droned on for an hour, and I think most of us just dozed, continuing our naps from Quiet Time. I couldn't sleep really, but I think I did nod off a few times, only to snap awake again when I felt Gavin move.

Eventually, Lars said, "And now, come back into your bodies, rise back into them. Feel yourself returning to your body."

I heard Gavin mutter, "Something is rising."

I couldn't help it, I snorted with laughter, quickly covering my mouth to stifle it.

Lars went on as though he hadn't heard us. "When you are ready, start wiggling your fingers and toes. Slowly start moving your limbs. Open your eyes. Again, only when you are ready, sit up."

Gavin and I sat up, having been ready since we started. We let go of each other's hands reluctantly.

Ella, though, was still flat on her mattress, wiggling her fingers. She blinked and opened her eyes, stretched, and sat up slowly. "That was wonderful!"

We laughed, and she frowned. "What's so funny?" She looked at the two of us and said, "Oh, you two. You didn't do it, did you?"

"Nah," Gavin said, and I shook my head.

Ella swatted at us both playfully. She wandered over to Lars to thank him, while Gavin leaned into me.

"What I said was, why don't we meet up in cabin one later?" He whispered it in my ear, but I still heard the promise in his words.

I froze and inhaled sharply. Cabin one, the empty cabin. The one where no one was allowed while it wasn't being used. I knew why Gavin would want to meet there. I'd heard the tittering of others about kids meeting up there.

"Can we get in there?"

"Don't worry about it."

"I don't know," I said, hesitating. Was I ready for this? Going alone to someplace deserted with a boy?

"Come on," he whispered.

I didn't say anything, not sure I was ready for that yet. Whatever "that" was going to be, I didn't want to think about it. I hadn't ever considered it could be a possibility.

Ella joined us then, saving me from having to answer. "That was wonderful!" she said again. "I'm glad we did it. And you two!" She looked us up and down. We were still holding hands, but I was feeling uncomfortable with it. She stepped a little closer to us and leaned in to ask quietly, "Are you sure you're okay?"

"We'll be fine," Gavin said.

I hoped he was right. I didn't want us to become the focus of some bigoted kid's crusade, with parents being "notified" of the possibility of two boys kissing. Ella had assured me there were plenty of queer kids here, but I hadn't seen any, except us.

Gavin was going to meet some other friends, so he hugged me, grabbed up his mattress, and ran off, leaving me alone with Ella. After we replaced our own mattresses, we went into Washington Lodge to find a place to talk. The back porch there was screened in and had a nice view of the steep hill. We had it to ourselves, as the afternoon activities were just finishing up, and the others hadn't come back yet. We settled into two deck chairs, leaning back to gaze out into the trees. Birds were flitting from branch to branch, twittering at one another.

"So? What's going on between you two?" Ella asked, her eyes shining with excitement.

"Nothing, it's nothing."

"Oh come on, you were holding hands, you hugged! That's something!"

I took a deep breath and let it out slowly. "He wants to meet in cabin one."

Ella's mouth opened into a big O of surprise. "Oh, my god, Casey, that's serious! Are you sure about that?"

"Honestly? No. I don't even know what, exactly, he wants to do there, but I don't think I'm ready for it, no matter what it is. I...I haven't kissed anyone seriously yet."

Ella knew that. She reached out and grabbed my hand to squeeze reassuringly. "You don't have to do anything you don't want to do."

"I know. I won't. It's just...I want to make sure he knows that."

"If he forces you to do something you don't want, you don't need him, no matter how cute he is," she said, clutching at my hand so hard it hurt.

"I know, I know. Ow." She let go with an apologetic look. "I don't want to get into any more trouble, I think."

"Then tell him, Casey. He should know you're already on thin ice."

"Yeah, because of Ryan," I said.

"Forget him. He's always been a creep."

"Gavin was friends with him."

"Only for a while. You said so."

I wanted to think Gavin was a nice guy—a real nice guy—but I couldn't help but feel a little squeamish about going into a cabin we weren't supposed to be in, to do things I wasn't sure I was ready for yet. I didn't want him to pressure me. I didn't want to have to push him away like that, but if he insisted, it would be for the best anyway. It was all moving too fast for me.

We still had a long time until dinner, so I decided to take a nap, as the "meditation" session had made me sleepy for real. I hugged Ella goodbye and went back to the cabin.

I stopped short when I realized Alex was the only one there. He glanced up at me, and his face froze into a look of contempt and anger.

"Look, Alex," I said, wanting things to be right again. He'd just started being friendly with us, and he had no other friends here. It wasn't right.

"Save it," he snapped.

"What's wrong?"

"Nothing."

I went over to him, my hands awkwardly thrust into my pockets. I didn't know what to say to him, but I didn't want him to hate me for something I wasn't sure I'd done. "I thought we were friends?"

"You were wrong."

"Why?"

He looked away, his jaw working. I was just about to give up when he took a big breath and went on a tirade at me. "It's you and Gavin! How could you like him? He's such a creep—he and Ryan always laughing at us behind our backs. You know their parents are friends, right? They went to the same school before Gavin moved away. How could you be attracted to him? What's wrong with you?"

I stared at him openmouthed as he finally lapsed into silence. He shook his head and stood up, but I was blocking his way. He went to push past me, but I had gathered myself up enough to stop him. I grabbed his arm. "What do you mean, they make fun of us?"

"You don't know?"

"No, how could I? Gavin said he didn't hang out with Ryan anymore, that they weren't really friends."

"He told you that? He was lying."

I didn't want to believe him. "How do you know this?"

"I overheard them. They were laughing about you." He hesitated. "Ryan knows you're trans. They were talking about how they could use it against you."

Fear rushed through my veins, a white wash of horror and dread that made me shiver. With numb lips, I said, "I don't believe you."

"Doesn't matter. Ryan wanted to tell a bunch of people. He told me, but I'd already guessed."

"That can't be true." I didn't want it to be true.

Alex slumped a little. "Sorry I didn't tell you sooner. I...I don't know why I didn't."

"No, it's okay. Um..."

Should I thank him? Should I scream at him? What if he was the one who was lying? But why would he lie? Why would Gavin lie? Why had Alex been okay with being friendly with him at first, only to decide against it when he saw us holding hands?

I knew the answers, but I didn't want to admit them.

I would have to find out myself. I would have to talk to Gavin, but I didn't want to do that.

He had said he was meeting with other friends, and I hadn't thought much of it. Gavin was attractive and nice, on the surface at least, so of course, he would have lots of friends. But what if those friends were Ryan and his cronies?

"Do you know where they hang out?" I asked.

"Yeah, cabin one."

I didn't want to believe Alex, but the coincidence of Gavin inviting me to cabin one and having his friends meet him there was worrying. Or maybe he could get access to cabin one because of Ryan?

I didn't know what to think anymore, and it was this state of mind that sent me creeping through the woods behind the cabins toward the other end of the road. I hadn't been back that way at all, but it wasn't hard to follow the line of the cabins. It was too hard to do it quietly.

Cabin one was set a little farther away from the line the other cabins were in, because the mountain reared up behind it and made it impossible to place it near cabin two. It had been set forward, closer to the road, and the road itself had petered out to a Jeep trail. There was no way for me to approach it quietly in the woods, so I went ahead and got back on the road. I slowed down, looking to see if anyone was coming but didn't see anything

I approached the cabin as quietly as I could, listening. There were voices inside, but I couldn't make out what they were saying, or even who they were.

Creeping closer, I tried to make as little sound as possible. It was good the road was dry, and the soft dirt muffled my footfalls.

"...bring...here..." I caught just that bit, but couldn't place the voice. I needed to see who it was, and there wasn't an easy way to do that. Not without opening the door or climbing the hill to peer into the screen windows. But with either option, they would be able to hear me approach.

"...doesn't...listen...tell everyone..."

Mumbling. I couldn't hear anything anymore. Someone must have turned away or started whispering.

"...hurt him...into...trouble..."

"...her, him, whatever..."

I grimaced. They had to be talking about me. Moving a bit closer, I stepped carefully onto the first step of the cabin. I hoped it wouldn't creak, and luckily, it didn't. But in concentrating on not making any sound, I'd missed a few sentences. Someone else said, "Do you really like her?" And then more mumbling.

Suddenly, there was laughter, and it was cruel. I knew that laugh. It was Ryan. But who else was in there?

The doors on all of the cabins were wooden, with a screen window set into the top half. Shades could be pulled down over the screen, and this one had been lowered. It was impossible to see in—there was no gap between shade and frame. I dared to peek, but could see nothing.

"...being around me." And then more laughter.

Finally, Ryan said as clear as day, "Bring her here, and you don't have to watch or participate. Just get her here."

There were footsteps. I needed to get away. They were going to come out! I panicked and ran straight into the woods.

The door flung open behind me, banging on the wall next to it.

"She's there!" Ryan yelled, and I could hear the shouting of the others.

I didn't look behind me to see who was coming out. I'd heard enough to know they were planning on hurting me, and that was all I needed to know. I had to get away.

Crashing through the trees, I headed straight for the rest of camp. I knew the only safe place would be with a crowd, and everyone would be getting ready for dinner soon. Branches slapped at my face, but I ignored them. Once past cabin two, I turned a sharp corner onto the road.

A couple of girls screamed as I nearly plowed into them. I threw a look behind me, and sure enough, Ryan and the other boys were pelting toward me. And behind them all was Gavin, running to catch up.

Anger swelled inside my gut like a balloon full of lava. I had trusted Gavin. I thought he really liked me. But it had all been an act, one to get me to follow him into cabin one and get beaten up. The betrayal stung, eating at my insides. What sort of person would do such a thing?

I skidded to a halt as I reached Washington Lodge, turning to face my pursuers. There was nothing they could do here, with this many people around.

"Just try it," I challenged. I glared at Gavin, letting him see the hate in my eyes. He wouldn't look at me, guilt written all over his face. Good, he should feel guilty, the asshole.

We stood there for a few tense moments, each staring at the other, until Ryan finally laughed and said, "Never mind, guys, we'll just let everyone know that Casey is really a girl."

There were enough people around that a few heard and turned to look at us.

This was it. I straightened and shook my head. "No, Ryan, you're wrong. I'm trans. I'm not a girl."

"Whatever. You're still a girl. You weren't born a boy. Freak." There were mutters from the people around us. They weren't friendly, but I couldn't tell if they were angry at me or at Ryan. He didn't seem sure, either, so he only gave me a dirty look. "Come on guys, let's leave the sissy alone." He turned and stalked off. Gavin went with him, the coward.

My hands had balled into fists without me realizing it. I relaxed them and ran a hand through my hair. Well, the secret was out. No sense hiding it now.

Chapter Five

I WENT BACK to the cabin where Wade was rounding everyone else up. Luckily, Ryan and his friends had stayed outside, gone off somewhere else. I told Wade what happened.

"Ryan found out I'm trans," I said, "and announced it in front of the lodge."

His face fell. "Oh, Casey, I'm sorry. Is there anything I can do?"

"Have Ryan thrown out?"

Wade's lips pressed down into a thin line. "You know how that will go,"

"Yeah, I know. Thought I'd try anyway."

He gripped my shoulder in sympathy, "Is there anything else I can do for you?"

"Can...can we just make an announcement at dinner?"

He looked surprised. "Really? You want to announce it?"

"I think it will be better than the rumors that are already probably spreading."

"You might be right. I'll put it on the list."

"Thanks."

We went to meet everyone else for the walk down to dinner. Alex was there, and I went straight up to him. "Thank you. You were right. They were planning to hurt me."

"Oh, man, really? I'm sorry." He looked stunned. He reached out and hesitantly touched my shoulder in sympathy. "I'm sorry, Casey."

"It's okay. I appreciate you telling me."

"I should have said something sooner."

"No, it's okay. I'm glad you did."

We picked back up the pieces of our friendship on the way back down the mountain to the dining hall. Once there, we sat with Ella, Nick, and Lily. I leaned over and whispered furiously to Ella what had happened. Her face whitened, her mouth dropping open in surprise, until she clenched it in anger.

"What an asshole," she hissed at me when I had finished. "Oh, I'm so sorry, Casey."

I also told her about the announcement I was going to make. She reached over and hugged me from the side, and our heads touched. She knew how hard this was going to be for me.

I tried my best to be "stealth." I was young and could easily pass as a young boy for the most part. But everyone at school already knew I was trans, so I wasn't really stealth there. I'd hoped I could be here, fitting in and passing without everyone noticing, without having to tell them. And I'd succeeded, mostly. But even being stealth, I would always be trans. It always meant the possibility of discovery, of being outed. To some people, me being trans meant I would never, ever be a real boy, no matter what I said or how I looked. They were wrong. Being trans didn't mean I wasn't a boy.

There was always a danger to being trans, a danger that never went away. I could be stealth, but if I did something "wrong," something too stereotypically girly, or if someone looked too closely, they might discover I was trans. My parents had not shied away from telling me of the violence and hardships some trans people encountered. They were real with me, sharing stories of trans people who'd been fired, beaten up, thrown out of their homes, had their children taken away from them, or had been murdered. It was terrifying. Some part of me hated my parents for showing me that. I was just a kid.

But it was my reality. It was what I could expect. My life wasn't going to be happy rainbows and accepting friends all the time, unfortunately. Ryan had illustrated that clearly. I needed to be ready, prepared for what could come in the future. When I'd come out, my parents hadn't sugarcoated it. As long as I was aware of what could happen, they would let me transition while I was still a kid.

We worked to change that. But so far, that was my reality.

Too nervous, I barely registered what I ate for dinner. The food was ashes in my mouth, dry and choking. Drinking a lot of bug juice helped wash it down, but I didn't taste that either. It all sat in my stomach like rocks. I only ate because I had to, because everyone else was, because Ella wouldn't leave me alone if I didn't.

After everyone had finished eating, there were a few announcements. I didn't hear any of them, but one of them made everyone murmur happily and clap. I'd have to check with Ella what it was later, once this was out of the way.

Wade stood then, and I knew it was time. My hands went cold and my heart was beating so hard I could feel it moving my whole body. Blood roared in my ears.

He licked his lips, looked at me, and said, "A situation has come up, and I'm sure some of you have heard the rumors. Casey has something to say."

I stood up, shaking. "Yeah, so, it's true, I'm trans. I'm a boy. So, please continue to treat me like a boy."

I sat back down, hadn't looked at anyone, hadn't seen their faces or their expressions. I couldn't say anything else, because my dinner was threatening a reappearance, and I wasn't sure I could survive the shame of that.

There were some murmurs, but no one laughed. Ella clutched my hand and squeezed it. I looked over and saw Ryan, whose face was contorted into a look of rage. I didn't want to look at Gavin, but I did anyway and noticed he was looking back at me. Our eyes met, and he was the first one to look away.

He was still sitting with Ryan. *Traitor. Liar.*

We were dismissed for Canteen, and I'd never gotten up the mountain faster. I didn't want to talk to anyone. I didn't even want a soda. I just wanted to be left alone—even left Ella behind, knowing she would understand.

The door to the cabin banged shut behind me, and I didn't even bother to turn the light on, just went to my bunk and got into bed. Sleep wasn't going to be possible, but I couldn't face anyone else.

I'd wanted so badly to pass, to be stealth, to not make this whole thing about me being trans. I wanted to live life like any other boy. It infuriated me that people like Ryan made being trans so hard, so dangerous. It didn't have to be. I could be like any other boy in just about every single way. It didn't matter what parts I did or didn't have. Our body parts didn't make us who we were. Why couldn't people treat others how they wanted to be perceived? Why was it such an issue with some people?

A while later, the door opened, creaking on its hinges. "Casey?"

I didn't respond, not sure who it was, and I didn't care.

"Oh, you are there." The light came on, and I blinked in the sudden brightness. It was Alex. "Are you okay?"

"I'm fine."

He walked over to my bunk, looking up at me. "Are you sure? Don't you want to have a soda?"

"Not really. I'm fine."

Alex hesitated. "Look, man, I know you're going through a lot. I was, too. You helped me, and now I'm gonna help you."

"What do you mean?"

"You talked to me. You were nice to me. You didn't have to be."

"Why wouldn't I have been?"

"Because I'm gay."

"You might have noticed, but I'm pretty bisexual," I said.

"Yeah, and that's cool."

"But I just had to out myself to the whole camp, and I didn't want to ever have to do that."

"I know. I know what it's like. Not to be able to be just a regular person. Me being gay means it's what most people think of when they talk to me. It can't be that I like games, or that I can play guitar, or anything else. It's that I'm gay."

I sat up. "Yeah. People always want to talk to me about being trans. It's annoying. I mean, it's like constantly asking someone to talk about one small aspect of their life and never being interested in anything else."

He smiled and nodded. "Exactly. So...do you want to talk about something else then?"

I had to laugh at that. He was right. I was letting this get to me. I was the one making everything be about me being trans. It had been fun just being a boy at camp. I could still do that—be like any other boy, show people I was like any other boy.

I hated being the person to do that for everyone else. They should accept that I was a boy and treat me like one. But maybe by knowing me, they'd treat the next trans person they met like anyone else: a full, whole, complete person.

I hopped off of my bunk and followed Alex out into the twilight. Ella joined us shortly after. I got myself a soda, but they had only grape left. That was okay, but it wasn't great.

The whole time, no one said anything to me about being trans. No one came up to me and said anything weird. I got a few smiles, a few nods, and a couple blank stares. But nothing else was said.

It made me feel a lot better.

OVER THE NEXT few days, everything went back to normal. If anyone other than Ryan had a problem with me being trans, no one said anything about it. More importantly, no one said anything to me about it. People were a little more polite, even those people I didn't know, but other than that, no one changed how they treated me.

In all honesty, it was a relief. I no longer ran to the bathroom to change. I just took off my pajamas, put on my binder, and then got dressed like everyone else. I still showered at night, because I didn't want to be accused of letting boys ogle me while I was naked, and I felt more comfortable that way anyway. My chest gave me such bad dysphoria that I wanted to be naked in front of others as little as possible.

Not believing my luck, I certainly didn't squander it, and went right back into having fun at camp like any other boy. I forgot about romance, forgot about Gavin. Of course, I still had to share the cabin with him and Ryan, and the other boys, but they left me strictly alone. It didn't matter to me that Gavin looked sullen and stopped hanging out with anyone. I'd often see him sitting alone, far away from everyone else. It served him right.

I hadn't come to camp to date. I had come to have fun, and that was exactly what I did. Not even Ryan loudly talking about how weird I was could dampen my day. No one was listening to him anyway, and I got special pleasure from seeing him being ignored by all the other kids. They might not be defending me, but they certainly weren't listening to him.

I signed up for the special overnight camping trip at the very top of the mountain. It was to be a daylong hike and an overnight stay. Alex and I wanted to go for it, but Ella—and Ryan—did not.

I had fun organizing my things to fit into a real backpack—those special ones with frames for carrying big loads—and tying my sleeping bag to it. We ate trail mix on the hike and cooked stew over the fire when we got there. We slept under the open sky, watching the stars wheeling above us with a clarity I'd never seen before. And I wondered at the Milky Way, spilled across the heavens, like a glass of milk poured across black. It was beautiful.

The next morning, we detoured to a waterfall that cascaded over several different levels and ended in a pool so cold no one could stand being in it long. But it was deep enough to jump into, and Alex and I watched from the edge as a couple of kids leaped in from one of the upper levels. We sat by the pool, taking in the beauty of the woods, the moss-covered rocks, and the white spray of the water as it fell over the lips of stone.

We also got first dibs on showers when we got back, which was a luxury.

Excitement was growing for the end of the session, which was packed with interesting activities. After the camping trip, there was the talent show, which was what everyone had been so excited about before I announced I was trans. Then there was some mysterious activity that the counselors were all excited about. And finally, there was the dance.

Already, people were pairing off, asking one another to the dance. I, of course, asked Ella again, formally, and she agreed to go with me as friends. She was excited about it, but I wasn't really. It was just a dance, and they were always a little boring in my experience. Especially here, where there was no chance of kissing anyone.

I was taken aback when a few of the girls shyly came up to me and asked if I wanted to go with them. I politely declined and told them I was already going with my best friend. I was flattered, but I just didn't want to get involved.

There was another pool party, and I was kind of sad I hadn't brought anything to swim in. So, instead of lamenting about it, I put on a shirt I didn't care about much, took off my binder, and jumped in. I didn't care, for once, that people could see my chest in outline. It had been so long since I'd gone swimming, other than just in my parents' pool, that it didn't bother me. Afterward, Ella and I chased the fireflies and sat by the fire to warm up. I roasted enormous molten marshmallows for her until everyone saw what I was doing and tried to copy me. Only a few people were able to roast them right. Most ended up setting fire to their marshmallows. I ate Ella's share of the chocolate, as well as mine.

By the time we started into the second week, I was thoroughly enjoying myself and couldn't believe there were only a few days left.

At breakfast one morning, Ella turned to me. "So are you going to do anything at the talent show?"

"Nah. You know I don't have any talents."

"Except roasting marshmallows," cut in Alex, who hadn't been able to successfully roast a single one. He kept getting impatient and got his too close the flames, lighting the marshmallow on fire.

I laughed. "Well, can't really do that on stage, can I?"

Ella leaned past me to stage-whisper to Alex, "Don't believe him, he's got a great singing voice."

"I do not!"

She gave me a look, one of those what-do-you-know looks. "You're just self-conscious about it."

"Well, yes."

"I play guitar, you know," Alex said. "We could always duet."

I stared at him, shocked that he'd suggest it.

"Oh, that would be wonderful!" Ella crowed. "You have to do it now. Come on, Casey!" She reached out and shook me a little.

"Okay, I guess." I was secretly pleased, though. I did like to sing, even if I wasn't fantastic at it.

In our free time, Alex and I got together to plan what we were going to do for the talent show. He didn't have his guitar with him, but Lars had a couple, and he let us borrow one of them under his watchful eye.

Unfortunately, Alex and I had widely varying tastes in music. But we managed to settle on a popular song we both knew, one that had been everywhere, so it was hard not to have heard it.

We practiced in between rounds of Greek dodgeball—which was a lot more fun when Ryan wasn't playing—nature hikes, and meals. Alex was actually pretty good at guitar, if a little bit slow at changing chords. We struggled at first and then picked up steam until we weren't too bad. I kind of hated my high-pitched voice, but since everyone now knew I was trans, it didn't matter so much.

The day before the talent show, we were given permission to use the back room of Washington Lodge to practice during Canteen.

"No, that chord is still wrong," Alex muttered to himself. He fingered it a few times, and then, satisfied he had it, we tried again.

"I think it's coming along," I said. "Are you ready?"

He hesitated for a moment, sliding his hand up and down the guitar neck. "Yeah." He looked back up at me. "I think so."

"Good. I think we'll do well."

We relaxed and finished off our sodas—I was still drinking grape soda since cabin eight hadn't yet won a Clean Cabin Award—before heading back to find Lars.

On our way out, Gavin stumbled into the room. He took one look at us, froze, reddened, and turned around, leaving quickly.

Alex and I shared a look.

"What a jerk," I said.

Alex shrugged. "I think he really does like you."

"Are you serious? You think I should get with him? After all that?"

"No!" Alex shook his head vehemently. "No way. He's a jerk. But I think he is gay, or bisexual. At least, no one's seen him with a girl."

"Doesn't mean much." I preferred boys, but I was still bisexual. "You think Ryan knows he's gay or whatever?"

"Probably. I mean, they were trying to get you into cabin one. They were using Gavin to bring you. Everyone saw you together, and people talk."

I felt sick at the thought.

"I don't know why they're still friends," I said. But I didn't care that much. If Gavin wanted to be friends with a homophobic wart like Ryan, that was his business. "Whatever."

We found Lars and gave him back his guitar. It was nearly bedtime, and both of us were tired. We sought out Ella, said goodnight, and went back to our cabin.

As I lay in my bunk, I thought about the talent show the next night. I was nervous, but I think we had a good shot. If we won, we'd be exempt from all the chores around camp, and we'd get pizza. I think I was more excited about the exemption, though Wade had relented on giving Ryan and me extra chores after I came out. That had been a relief, but we still hadn't won the Clean Cabin Award. Wade was inconsolable. I mean, we weren't slobs, but I guess the other cabins were just doing that much better than us. It was disappointing.

Nerves kept me awake for a while, but so did the thought that Gavin still liked me. I turned over. I didn't want him. He was a jerk. He hung out with Ryan, though admittedly I hadn't seen them together in a long time. Not since my coming out.

I told myself people did not change. Not unless they wanted it. Mom had drilled that into my head when I started even thinking about dating. She'd had an abusive husband before she met my dad. That bastard had nearly killed her, but she'd stayed with him anyway, thinking and hoping he could change.

She managed to finally leave him in the end, but she made sure I knew it wasn't worth staying with a jerk just because you loved him.

I didn't love Gavin. I'd just crushed on him. That made me angry, which made it harder to sleep. He'd lied to me about still being friends with Ryan, about being okay with me being trans, and he had tried to lure me into cabin one to get me beaten up. What kind of person does that?

Sleep finally did come, but not good sleep. I dreamed a lot about Gavin, which woke me up a few times during the night. Why was I dreaming about him? He was off-limits. I reminded myself he wasn't going to change. I couldn't make him, and holding out hope would only bring pain and heartache later. But it was hard to believe when he was sleeping just underneath me. If I dared peer down over the edge of the bunk, I would see his face in the moonlight. His brow would be creased while he slept, his pale lashes on his freckled cheeks.

I rolled over again and tried to sleep, trying to think of other things than Gavin's eyelashes.

Chapter Six

THE MORNING DAWNED a little cool, and I shivered into my clothes as quickly as possible. It would warm up once the sun broke through the clouds and the wind died down. But it must have rained during the night, for the ground was a little soggy.

I ran to the bathroom and came back to everyone in the cabin starting the day. As we did our chores, Gavin, Ryan, and I studiously ignored one another. Ryan's face was always set, as though he wanted to spit at me or yell at me, but he'd frozen it instead so as not to show how much he hated me. Gavin kept letting his eyes wander to me, and then he would look away quickly. I could sometimes feel his eyes on my back or see him staring at me out of the corner of my eye, but I ignored him.

We took extra care with the chores, and Wade's inspection was still harsh. He yelled at Ryan for a few creases in his sheets. He pointed out a few spots of dust I'd missed. Satisfied we had cleaned enough, he let us line up for breakfast.

As I left, I felt a hand on my shoulder. Someone trod on my heels, and I turned and saw Gavin. I gave him a dirty look. "What?"

"Can you just talk to me for a second?"

"No, I can't."

His face fell, but he reached out and grabbed my shirt as I began to walk away.

"Let go of me," I ordered him.

He did, but I turned and crossed my arms over my chest. "What?"

He steeled himself. "I just thought you should know the truth."

"About what?"

Gavin flicked his eyes to the other boys, who were passing by us with curious glances thrown in our direction. They undoubtedly wanted to listen in. Once they were gone, he said, "About what Ryan was planning."

"I don't want to know."

"No, I mean about me."

"What? That you were baiting me? That you were going to lure me in to get hurt? That you lied about being friends with him? That you lied about being okay with me being trans? Save it, Alex told me the truth."

It was satisfying to watch the blood drain from his face. With bloodless lips he said, "No, that's not what I was doing. I wasn't going to do it. I didn't think that..."

"Really?" I was unconvinced.

"Yes, really," he said, anger suddenly transforming his face. "Ryan was ordering me to do it, otherwise he would out me to my parents. My dad..." He slammed his mouth shut, but I caught a quiver of his lip.

"And I should care?"

"Because I wasn't going to do it!" He half shouted it and looked around furtively to make sure no one had heard him. "You must not have heard the part where I was arguing with him."

It was true I hadn't heard the entire conversation. Ryan had been the loudest speaker, and I'd only made out what he'd said and mumbles from everyone else. But it didn't matter. "You should have told someone about it. I could have been hurt. You lied to me."

"I know! I didn't get a chance to tell anyone! That was the first time he'd said anything about doing…that. And I hadn't lied…just…"

I didn't want to let him finish the excuse. I didn't care why he and Ryan had been making fun of me. "Why were you hanging around him anyway?"

"Because he was my only friend for a long time. He's an asshole, but he's sometimes nice."

"Gavin, that's not a reason to stay friends with people," I said. "That's called abuse, you know? And why would you laugh along with him when he made fun of me? Of me being trans?"

He whitened again, his freckles standing out starkly against his pale skin. I felt empathy creeping in, and I didn't want it. I felt bad for him—that he stayed with someone who was clearly abusing him, blackmailing him, but he had allowed it. He'd enabled Ryan's bad treatment of others, was a bystander to their pain. He had laughed along with him, even though he knew it was wrong.

"I know," he mumbled. "But I don't have anyone else."

"I wonder why?"

I was done with this conversation. I pushed past him and went to join the others. Almost everyone had lined up to go down the mountain, and I found Wade and Alex and stuck by them rather than be anywhere near Gavin, who moped along after me.

At breakfast, Alex, Ella, and I sat together. Lily and Nick were sitting with some other friends, so we had our side of the table to ourselves. To my consternation, Gavin sat down at the end of the table, a few seats away. Damn him.

"Are you ready for tonight?" Ella asked brightly as she passed me a croissant and then the butter.

I looked at Alex, who nodded. "I think so," I replied. "If we can get in one more practice, we'll be good."

"Do you think they'll let us skip afternoon activities?" Alex asked. "Or Quiet Time?"

Ella shrugged. "Activities aren't required. I mean, they're strongly encouraged, because the counselors have to keep an eye on people in groups. But I think if Lars is with you, you don't have to do activities."

We planned on that, vowing to check with Lars after breakfast to see.

After the meal, the morning activity we all signed up for was watercolor painting. I thought it would be boring, but Ella and Alex had both wanted to do it, so I went along with them.

We set up at the tables in Lincoln Lodge, and it was Angela again who was the counselor for the morning. She passed out paper and paint sets. It was then I noticed Gavin was there, too.

I nudged Ella and pointed him out. "He's been trying to get back into my good graces," I whispered.

She looked over, saw Gavin, and frowned. "What's he been doing?"

"He tried to tell me the 'truth' about what he and Ryan had been planning."

"Well, was it the truth?" Ella asked. Alex was watching us with wide eyes, leaning in so he could hear our whispered conversation.

"How can you say that?" I stabbed my brush into the water and then into the red paint. We were supposed to do whatever came to mind, and all I could think about was how angry I was at Gavin. And now Ella might be defending him?

"Well, you did only hear part of the conversation," Ella said, and I suddenly wanted to be anywhere else other than here. How could she be saying this to me?

"So?"

"So? What if he is telling the truth?"

"Then he's an asshole for not saying something to someone about it."

"Did he have a chance? Did he say he was going to turn Ryan in?"

I jabbed my brush into the yellow, not caring I had smeared a big streak of red into it. I didn't answer.

Ella eyed me, clucking her tongue. "Casey, I know this mood. You didn't even give Gavin a chance, did you?"

"Why should I?"

My voice was getting too loud, and a couple people, including Gavin, looked over at me. In a lower voice, I asked it again, "Why should I?"

"Because it's the right thing to do?" Ella said, and Alex nodded.

"I don't believe this. You're defending him! Both of you."

"No, I'm not," Ella slammed her brush down and glared at me. "If Gavin knew that Ryan was going to hurt you, and was going to turn him in, that's something. You interrupted their meeting. You didn't give Gavin a chance to explain. You didn't even give him a chance to apologize to you."

"They were going to beat me up for being trans, Ella. I don't need an apology from him. Ryan and Gavin were laughing about me being trans. Alex heard them."

Alex squirmed in his seat.

"An apology from Ryan, no, you don't need that. But if Gavin wasn't going to be involved, then you've vilified him for no reason." She turned to Alex and asked, "Did you actually hear Gavin say those things, or was he just there when Ryan said them?"

I couldn't believe this. Before Alex could answer, I said, "Vilified?"

Sometimes I hated Ella for always being so reasonable, for sounding so adult. Occasionally, she acted more like a parent than a friend, and those were the only times we ever fought. It looked like this was going to be one of those times.

"Yes, vilified. He likes you, Casey. You can still see it. I mean look at him." She waved her brush in his direction. I didn't look. "If he said that he was going to turn in Ryan, then maybe he was. Maybe Ryan pulled him in against his will."

Gavin had said as much, but the nasty part of me didn't want to admit that to Ella. It would only prove her point and make her even more insufferable. I stayed silent, loathing myself for it. But damn it, I wanted to be mad at Gavin. I wanted to hate him. He'd betrayed me and lied to me. It was quite possible he hadn't been planning on turning Ryan in, but I had no proof.

Ella knew I was holding something back. She narrowed her eyes at me and set her jaw in that way I knew so well. We could read each other like books, and she saw the deception written all over my face. I felt my skin burn in a blush.

"Why do you hate him so much?" Ella shook her head, apparently meaning it as a rhetorical question, because she turned away and concentrated on her painting. She was done with the conversation, and from the set of her shoulders, I knew I wouldn't be able to argue with her further.

My painting had become a spreading mess of red, orange, and yellow paint. It felt strangely symbolic.

WE HAD LUNCH and then set it up with Lars to practice during Quiet Time. Unfortunately, the only place where we could meet was cabin one. Both lodges were being used for afternoon activities, so they were off-limits as the counselors set up for them. We obviously couldn't practice in our cabin, where everyone was resting.

So we trooped down to cabin one, which was far enough away we shouldn't disturb anyone. Alex and I followed Lars as he unlocked the door and let us in.

I half expected it to be scary or creepy, considering what Ryan had wanted to do to me there, but it was just another cabin. There were only four bunks instead of five, and they held only bare mattresses. There was a closet that was open but empty as well. It was like any of the others, only deserted. Everything was dustier, though, as it obviously hadn't been cleaned in a while. Footprints marred the carpet of dirt on the floor.

Lars, who was wearing a fluffy green cardigan and violently orange corduroy pants, actually had some good pointers as he listened to us practice. I'd thought we were doing pretty well, but now we sounded downright good. If only my voice were deeper...

After Quiet Time, we were allowed to skip our afternoon activities as long as we stayed in our own cabin. I'd considered it, because I was still mad at Ella, but decided I could use some dodgeball to work off some steam.

I bid Alex goodbye, since he was going to go nap, and trekked down the mountain once more. The field was already full of kids starting up a tug-of-war game, and the pavilion was also full. A lot of people had signed up for dodgeball, and I wondered if we had too many to play effectively.

To my annoyance, Gavin was already there. I nearly turned around and walked back up the mountain. But if I could get on the opposite team from him, then it would be an excuse to chuck a ball at him. It wasn't very nice, but at least it would make me feel better.

But Gavin maneuvered himself to be on the same team as me. I decided to ignore him. A few times when I was in jail, though, he threw the ball straight to me. I considered just letting someone else throw the ball, but my competitive side wouldn't let me.

Why was he making this hard?

I think I knew the answer, because Ella had said it. He really did like me.

Which did not make me feel better.

People don't change. Gavin had shown he was more willing to keep a jerk like Ryan as a friend than stand up to him. It didn't matter if Gavin was gay or bi, he was still hanging around people like Ryan, who hated people like him. While it was possible he hadn't laughed about me being trans, he surely hadn't protested when Ryan had. That was just as bad.

I wasn't about to involve myself with someone like him just because he was cute. My mother's hard-fought lesson had taught me something. Abusers didn't change.

But the thought nagged at me that Gavin wasn't an abuser.

He was the abused.

That thought stopped me in my tracks, and I got hit with a dodgeball in the moment of my inattention. I went to the jail on the other side of the court, stunned in more than one way.

How many times had I, myself, kept silent when someone said something stupid, or mean, or phobic? It was easier to stay quiet, to not rock the boat, to not challenge your friends. Gavin was queer, so it was all too likely the only friends he had were the phobic ones. He might have managed to find another group of queer people at his school, if there were any. But he lived in a small town in West Virginia. There might not be any other out queers. We tried to hunt each other down, desperate to be around people who understood us. But for some, there might be no one. Or there was no way they could be out and open and hang with the other queer people without serious risk. Kids were still disowned, beaten up, or worse, by their families for being queer.

If Gavin was still closeted to his family, then perhaps his only choice was to be friends with the homophobes. Especially if their parents knew each other. He would be expected to hang out with someone like Ryan. It was like camouflage: do what you could to fit in and not stand out, otherwise be a target yourself.

I remembered Jessie, one of my friends from back home. He'd been one of the homophobes, laughing at all us queers. Until one day, he shyly approached Ella and asked her about a book she was reading. It was about being trans, and she gave it to him on the spot. While Jessie wasn't trans, he did realize he was queer, and that book changed his life. He repudiated the haters and joined the rest of us, and became quite a good friend.

He had told me of the intense struggle he had with being a queer boy. His parents expected him to perform masculinity perfectly: he was a strong athlete, had a string of pretty girlfriends even at his young age, was competitive in grades and everything else. But he'd hated every second of dating, which was why he'd been so bad at it. He liked sports, but he was distracted all the time because he was too busy making sure he didn't look too long at the other guys, or that no part of his personality or look came off as queer.

His word for it all had been "exhausting." It was a performance, all the time, for everyone. When he found us, he was finally able to relax into being his real self. His parents nearly threw him out when they found out, calling him all sorts of names and stating that no son of theirs could ever be a "sissy."

But they came around, and now, Jessie was comfortable and happy. But it had been terribly hard for him to break it off with those former friends. It had taken him all of one year to finally tell them to shut up when they said something homophobic, even after he'd borrowed that book from Ella. He wasn't friends with them anymore, but at least he'd stood up and at last said This is Not Acceptable.

Maybe Gavin was still like Jessie. Maybe he didn't know how to break away from Ryan. Maybe he didn't know how to come out to his parents.

Or maybe I was making excuses for him.

I had to think about that some other time. The game was starting to wind down, and I was still stuck in jail. I finally accepted a ball from another camper, but missed my target. Gavin tossed me yet another one, and that time, I made it out.

I don't know why, but I smiled at him and thanked him.

Chapter Seven

THE TALENT SHOW was after dinner, during Canteen. I had nothing to wear, because I hadn't anticipated performing or doing anything where I'd need a costume or fancy clothes.

Alex did have a nice jacket and a pair of nice jeans but didn't have any spares. Plus, he was a lot taller than me. I would never have fit into anything of his.

I had T-shirts and shorts, and my one pair of jeans were kind of faded. They would have to do, as well as my nicest T-shirt. I only hoped I wouldn't look like a total loser up on the stage.

I was so nervous I had a hard time getting my binder back on after having removed it for dodgeball and a shower. My fingers kept shaking and slipping on the fabric, and I almost punched myself in the face once. But I wrestled myself back into it at last and managed to get dressed.

I didn't talk much during dinner, which had Ella worried. I could see it in her face. And I barely ate, even though both she and Alex tried to feed me. It was all I could do to choke down a butt bun, but that was all. And after drinking too much bug juice, I had to go to the bathroom again.

We were going to the theater right after dinner, and as we trooped out of the dining hall, Lars caught up to us. He wore a flowered muumuu with his hiking boots, and was sporting pink lipstick and eyeliner. He handed Alex the guitar, ignoring the snickers from Ryan and his friends, and then hurried off to lead the procession of kids.

"Those guys are such jerks," Alex said, shaking his head. "I think Lars looks great."

"Yeah," I said.

While I couldn't agree with the "great," I did think it was good that Lars was wearing whatever he wanted. But the muumuu was too much. I thought he looked silly in it, but it was his body, not mine. He could do what he wanted with it.

We arrived at the theater and were allowed into the dressing room to wait for the show. I was nervous because they hadn't given us time to rehearse in the space. It was small, though, with a tiny stage at one end. There weren't even any real chairs. Most of the kids would be sitting on the floor, though there were a few scattered couches, school-type desk and chair combinations, and a few rickety old seats of the kind where you could peel the metal off in strips from the legs. At least there was actual lighting in the place, though I didn't have any stage makeup to wear. I didn't think the lights would be turned up enough to matter, and it wasn't a big show anyway.

Alex and I sat, fretting, in the green room while we waited for everyone to arrive.

Lars came back with cans of sodas for us. "Once you're done, you can sit in the audience," he said as he handed me the can. "You should make sure to watch the show and support the other participants."

"Thanks," I said, meaning it. That was a good idea. Maybe it was because I was doing it, but it took a lot of guts to get up in front of a bunch of other kids and perform. I was so nervous I couldn't taste the soda, even though it was one of my favorites.

I realized then I didn't even know who had won the Clean Cabin Award. I'd been too preoccupied to pay much attention to anything else. It likely wasn't us, or Wade would have said something. I guessed we got sodas first because we were performing, and everyone else would have to wait their turn as usual.

I wished I could see Ella before I performed, but I knew she was still mad at me. I was still kind of mad at her, too. But we never stayed angry with each other long, and this wasn't that big of a deal. At least I kept telling myself it wasn't.

I probably wouldn't ever see Gavin again after camp, so who cared if he liked me? Who cared what the truth was? In a few days, it wouldn't matter. I kept telling myself that, too.

We were on third, as Lars informed us, which was a huge relief. I wanted to get it over with as soon as possible. I didn't like the queasy feeling that had settled in my stomach, and the soda wasn't helping it.

I finished my soda without even realizing I'd been drinking it. I hoped I wouldn't belch on stage while I was singing. That was a lot of soda in a short amount of time. *Oops...*

Lars wandered back and told us we'd start in five minutes. When he opened the door, we could hear the crowd. The other performers had arrived, and the volume inside the dressing room had risen. Excitement was in the air, but all I could think about was how nervous I was.

And about Gavin.

I couldn't do this.

I suddenly didn't want to go on stage and have him watch me sing. He'd be in the audience, of course. I wanted to back out, but Alex had been working so hard. I couldn't disappoint him. And Ella. She tried so hard to be supportive of me singing, because she knew how hard it was for me to do it.

Before I knew it, it was our turn. I was shaking, but I didn't have time to think about anything anymore. Lars hustled us up to the stage, and suddenly we were under the bright lights. I blinked under their glare, the audience all but invisible to me. But I could see and hear Ella cheering, sitting as close to the stage as she could get.

Alex started playing and I started singing. We didn't have microphones, but the acoustics in the tiny theater were surprisingly good. We didn't need them.

Alex did a wonderful job, and before I knew it, I was smiling and having fun. I belted out the lyrics, getting into it. I loved music, loved singing, and I was doing it in front of everyone who knew I was trans. I forgot all about my insecurities about my voice. My binder didn't seem to hinder me at all. On that stage, I was just a boy singing a song about a girl, and having the time of my life. Everyone was clapping along, and the few people I could see were mouthing the lyrics along with me.

I held the last note as long as I could, the sound of Alex's guitar ringing in harmony, and then we were drowned out by thunderous applause. It kind of startled me, and I had to look back at Alex—who looked just as a stunned—to check if it was real. But it was. Ella had leapt to her feet, screaming my name and laughing her head off, and everyone else was clapping so hard.

I grabbed Alex's hand, and we took a bow together and then hurried off of the stage. The audience was still clapping; I couldn't believe it.

Lars was clapping too, smiling at us like he was our proud dad. "Great job, you guys! That was your best one!"

"Thanks!" we said together, in unison, and then shared a laugh. Alex and I hugged after Lars had taken his guitar back and headed to the stage to announce the next act.

"That was fantastic!" Alex told me.

"You were!"

"No, I mean you—you were really great."

"And so were you!" I didn't know how to take the compliment, so I gave him one in return.

We glowed at each other a little bit, hugged again, and went back to the dressing room to relax. The other kids politely asked us how it went, but I knew they'd heard the applause we'd received. We might just win this show, and they knew it.

My heart swelled in my chest. It would be perfect to win. It would be exactly what I needed. But I told myself firmly I didn't have to win to have had a good time, that winning wasn't everything. We hadn't seen the rest of the show, and it was entirely possible someone else would blow us out of the water.

But I hoped that didn't happen.

Alex and I got some water and then left the dressing room to go sit and be the audience for the rest of the show. Ella snuck back to join us in the rear of the theater. She crushed me in a hug, and when the next act was being announced, she whispered, "I am so proud of you both! That was amazing! You'll definitely win."

I couldn't thank her properly because of the next act coming on, but I was feeling all warm and fuzzy inside. Maybe I could still sing. I'd have to see what testosterone did to my voice once I started taking it, but I was more hopeful now. And I was happy Ella was speaking to me again. I was still a little mad at her for defending Gavin, but I couldn't live without her.

We watched the next few acts, recognizing each from backstage. Most of them were singers, belting along to recorded rather than live music. I felt grateful to Alex for being there with me, for being pretty awesome on the guitar.

At the end of the show, Lars came out onto the stage. But he didn't ask for us to come back up. Instead, he said, "We have one last act for you! They signed up late, but we decided to go ahead and let them perform. Please, everyone welcome Gavin!"

Oh. I clapped politely as he came onto the stage, his red hair shining under the lights. He looked genuinely frightened to be there, squinting against the glare and searching the audience.

In a clear voice, though it shook noticeably, he said, "This one is for someone special. He'll know who it is."

There was some murmuring and titters at the pronoun. I froze. Ella was staring at me; I could feel the weight of her gaze on my skin like a blanket. Alex's hand was on my shoulder.

In a high, clear voice, Gavin started singing a popular love song. He wasn't that great, but he also wasn't the worst we'd seen that night. And he was singing a cappella. There was nowhere for his voice to hide. I tried to focus on that and not on my embarrassment.

The song was about a love lost and regained, and as he sang, he scanned the audience, sweeping his gaze back and forth. I knew he couldn't see back this far into the audience because of the glare of the lights, and I was glad. He was looking for me.

My feelings tore at my insides. I wanted to disappear and never show my face again. I wanted to run up and hug him. I wanted to run away and never look back.

But I couldn't feel all those things at once, so I just sat staring at him as he sang his heart out, and let each emotion wash over me. Something was glimmering on his face, and with a start, I realized it was tears. He was singing about getting his love back, sorry for everything he'd done— *Won't you please take me back?*

I put my head into my elbows, resting them on my knees, and stared at the floor. My face was hot, and I was too mortified to look at him. And angry.

Did he think singing me a song, in public like this, was going to magically make me fall in love with him?

Ella was shaking me, and I looked up to see that he'd finished, and he was standing there uncertainly as everyone clapped for him. I hastily clapped, not really wanting to, but not wanting to be a jerk who didn't clap for someone. He'd done a decent job and deserved the recognition.

He staggered off the stage, and Lars came out again. "All right, let's get all of our contestants back up on stage!"

Alex and I went up together, weaving our way through the crowd. Everyone was applauding again, so Lars had to calm them down enough to be heard.

He went down the line, holding his hand over our heads and calling out our names, while the audience applauded for who they liked best.

When he got to Alex and me, the applause was definitely the loudest. Ella was screaming. I could hear her in the back, and it made me smile. They were still clapping as Lars tried to move on, and I couldn't believe it. I thought we'd won.

But Lars still went down the line. The other contestants all got polite applause at least, but many of them got more than that. Alex and I still had the loudest, though. It was easy to tell.

I clapped for Gavin as Lars got to him, even if it made me feel all weird inside—guilty and proud all rolled into one.

"All right!" Lars said. "I think we know who the winner is!" He came back over to us and shook my hand and then Alex's. "Casey and Alex! Congratulations you guys!"

There was a lot of applause then, people cheering for us, being happy for us. I caught sight of Gavin with a big grin on his face as I hugged Alex. His smile made him look even better, and I hated myself a little for thinking that.

People were slapping us on our backs and hugging us. I tried to keep myself away from Gavin, but he cornered me at one point. He only shook my hand and said, "You were amazing. Both of you." And then he left. I stared after him, shocked and disappointed that he'd gone so abruptly. He hadn't even mentioned his song to me.

Had it been for me?

What a ridiculous thought. Why was I doing this to myself?

Wade and Lars rounded everyone up soon after that, hustling us out of the theater. It was past our usual lights-out time, which made the show seem that much more enjoyable. We weren't technically breaking the rules, but it felt that way.

The walk back up the mountain was filled with laughter and shrieking in the dark. Ella and I walked hand in hand.

"I'm so proud of you," she told me. "See? I told you; you can sing."

"I know, I know. I'm just self-conscious about my voice."

"I know you are, and you shouldn't be."

"But it should be dropping by now."

It wouldn't though, not until I got on testosterone. The familiar feeling of disappointment and need warred within me. I wished my parents would relent on allowing me to get on hormone replacement therapy. I wanted to grow up into a boy. It was true, my implant would keep me from going further into puberty the way a girl would, but I wanted to go through it as a boy, with everyone else.

Ella's arm snaked around my shoulders, and she shook me gently. "Don't do that. Don't get all melancholy now."

"I can't help it. It takes up so much of my life, of my... brain space."

"I know. I'm sorry, Casey. But enjoy this, okay? Or try to?"

She was right. I needed to enjoy the good things, or I'd drive myself into another panic attack. Trying not to think about it, I changed the subject and brought Alex into it.

"So, thinking of continuing with the guitar?" I asked him.

He laughed a little. "Yeah, I guess so."

"Do you think you can? I mean, really get somewhere with it?"

"I hope so."

Ella said, "You were wonderful, Alex. I don't see why not?"

"I'm just not sure I can afford it," he said. "Lessons are expensive. My family doesn't want to pay for them—" he dropped his voice "—because they're a waste of time and money, better spent elsewhere." He rolled his eyes, a long-suffering expression on his face. He must have heard that a lot from his father.

"I'm so sorry, Alex," Ella said. "I wish more people valued the arts. They're so important."

I poked Ella. "Don't get started on your soapbox. Alex is the choir, right?"

She laughed self-consciously, rubbing at the spot where I'd poked her. "Yeah, you're right. I know. But they're important, right? I mean, we need art."

"Of course we do," I said, nudging Alex with an elbow. He grinned at us, and Ella sighed.

We finally reached the top of the mountain, and Ella bid us goodnight. We followed Wade back to the cabin, but I realized I needed to use the bathroom again before going to bed. I ran back to the latrines.

I didn't even think about it, just crashed the door open.

There was Gavin, surrounded by his old friends. I scowled before I realized something was very wrong.

Ryan had Gavin by the shirt, his arm pulled back and his hand in a fist. It looked like he was drawing back to punch Gavin. Gavin was trying to pry Ryan's fingers off of him, but he wasn't succeeding. They all turned to stare at me, freezing me in my tracks. All I could see was the fear in Gavin's eyes. Real fear.

"Get her!" Ryan shouted.

I turned and ran, adrenaline making me swift.

They thundered behind me, but I was faster and smaller.

I hit the nearest cabin door, not caring whose it was, and started banging on it, yelling, "Help!" Frightened voices erupted from within, but I didn't stop. I ran on to the next cabin, banging on the walls as I passed.

Soon, I'd roused half the camp, kids and counselors spilling out of the cabins in their pajamas. I ran until I got to Wade, who was storming out of our cabin.

"What is the meaning of this?" he demanded.

I pointed to where Gavin had come out of the bathrooms, pointing and yelling that Ryan had assaulted him there.

Meanwhile, Ryan and his friends had been caught trying to run away. Angela, whose cabin I'd first encountered, had a heavy hand on Ryan's shoulder. Another counselor had grabbed the other boys.

"What's going on?" Wade demanded again.

I was out of breath, but I gasped out, "I went to the bathroom and found Ryan and his friends trying to hurt Gavin."

Gavin pushed forward and said, "They did hurt me." He pulled up his shirt, exposing a pale belly devoid of freckles and a huge developing bruise on his chest.

Wade's eyes widened. He grabbed both of our shoulders and steered us toward Angela. Ryan's face held fear and anger, one emotion chasing the other across it.

Ella thrust through the crowd, pointing her finger accusingly at Ryan. "And he won't leave me alone! He's been harassing me!"

We all turned as she blurted it out. But then she faced me. "I didn't tell you before."

"He was still asking you out, even after you told him to stop?"

"Yeah."

"I'm sorry, Ella."

Wade had been watching with growing anger showing on his face. "Come with me," he said, and Angela made sure the other boys followed him. He flicked on a flashlight as all of us—Ryan and his friends, Angela, Wade, Ella, Gavin, and me—went right back down the mountain.

No one said anything the entire time. We could all hear the nighttime sounds of the forest, the sleepy tweets of the birds and the singing of the crickets. The only other sound was us tripping over rocks in the dark. It was awkward and scary walking in the night with only one flashlight. I didn't know where we were going.

I couldn't really see Gavin, but I could feel his gaze on me.

All I could think about was seeing the terror in his eyes as Ryan held him, his fist poised to hit him again. That, and the implications of it.

We got down to the field, but instead of continuing on, Wade steered us to the nurse's house. He knocked politely on the door, and it was quickly opened. The elderly nurse answered, flustered at the late-night interruption. Her hair was coming out of its tight bun in white wisps.

"What on earth is going on?" she asked. "Is anyone hurt?" Her eyes flicked to each of our faces, seeming to gauge for pain.

"I want you to check Gavin," Wade said, hustling us inside past her. "He's hurt."

"I'm fine," Gavin protested, but the nurse crooked her finger and made him follow.

"I need to use your phone," Wade called after her, and she waved her permission before disappearing with Gavin.

Wade and Angela pulled us all into the nurse's living room, and Wade said, "Sit." We did as we were told, scattering to the couch, a winged armchair, and the floor.

The counselors decided Angela would stay with us and make sure we didn't cause any more trouble. Wade made the call, but as the phone was in a different room, we had no idea what he said, or who he was calling. I could guess, though. It was too good to be true, so I didn't want to say it and spoil it. But I was hoping Ryan's parents would finally have to come and pick him up, throwing him out of camp for good. Or at least for the little we had left.

We all sat in uncomfortable silence, trying not to look at one another. Ryan's body was hunched, his arms crossed over his chest, his eyes burning holes into the floor. I could see his jaw grinding as he muttered to himself. His friends looked more worried than angry, flicking significant glances at each other. I wondered if they were going to set Ryan up for the bigger fall.

After a few minutes, the nurse brought Gavin into the living room. He was holding an ice pack wrapped in a towel to his chest but seemed fine otherwise. I felt my heart lurch in relief.

Without looking at anyone, Gavin sat down as far from everyone as he could.

I was getting sleepy, despite all the excitement. It had been a long day, and a lot had happened. But I couldn't sleep now, so I kept pinching myself to stay awake.

But then Ella stood up, glaring at Ryan. "I just want you to know, Ryan, that I'm not a freak. That there's nothing wrong with me."

He twisted his face up and opened his mouth to say something, but she interrupted him. "I'm asexual. I don't want to date. I especially don't want to date you."

"Then you *are* a freak," he blurted out, spit flying from his mouth.

"I am not!"

I wanted to stand up and defend my friend, but this was her fight. She'd been so worried about being asexual and how she might be broken. If she'd finally worked it out that she was perfect just the way she was, then she could defend herself.

"There's nothing wrong with being ace," she said. "I like it. I like just being friends with people. If you can't understand it, that's your problem."

Ryan snorted but wouldn't look at her, shaking his head.

"I know what you're thinking," Ella continued. "And you're not so special. You're just a bully with low self-esteem. You have no real friends, not like me." Ella grabbed my hand, squeezing it so hard it brought tears to my eyes. But I wasn't going to make her let go.

"Fuck you—"

"Enough!" Angela covered up whatever insult he was about to hurl at Ella. "Ryan, don't you dare use that language here. Ella, please sit down. It's inexcusable that Ryan has been bothering you."

"Bothering?" Ella scoffed. "He's been harassing me. I'll be filing a complaint."

Ryan's leg started jiggling, and he was now very pale. Good. He needed to have some fear of reprisal put into him.

We all subsided into silence, and Ella settled down next to me, still clutching my hand.

A few minutes longer and Wade finally came back into the room. He sat down on one of the last chairs available.

"I've called your parents, Ryan, Gavin. They're going to be here in the morning." He nodded to each of them. "Now, Gavin, would you mind telling me what happened?"

"Please don't make me tell my parents," he exclaimed. "Please don't!"

Wade didn't even blink. He said, "Gavin, you need to tell me what happened."

He was about to protest, but the look Wade gave him made him change his mind. "I was going to the bathroom—" He gulped and wagged a finger at Ryan and his friends. "—and they attacked me. Casey came in and stopped them."

"Well, I just interrupted," I said, and Wade shot me a quieting glance. I clamped my mouth shut.

"Yes," Gavin agreed. "Casey came in and interrupted them. Ryan was threatening to punch me in the face." He licked his lips. "He said something I'm not going to repeat, calling me gay and saying that I deserved to die."

"That's a very serious charge," Wade said.

"It's what he said." Gavin's voice rose, and then he looked at his hands and said in a dead voice, "I am gay. My parents don't know."

Ryan couldn't contain himself. A slur escaped his sneering lips, and suddenly everyone was up screaming. Wade had to push Ryan back into his chair, and Angela stood up to place herself in front of Gavin. Ryan's shouts could be heard over them all. "I've had to share a cabin with those two freaks!" and "I'm being discriminated against! This is against my religion!"

"Shut up!" Wade shouted over them all, and an ugly silence fell. "You will not use such language in front of me or anyone else." His voice was so cold I almost expected to see icy steam escape his lips.

"I already warned him," Angela told Wade.

Ryan's expression was full of malice and hate, and I wondered where he'd learned such emotions. Who had taught him to hate people so early?

Wade turned to the nurse, who'd been standing watching it all with pursed lips and folded arms. "Did Gavin look like he'd been punched?"

"There was a fist-shaped bruise on his chest, yes," she said. "But I'm no forensic scientist."

"You don't have to be." Wade turned to Ryan, who was still glaring at the floor, his nostrils flared wide. "You've been warned about starting fights already, Ryan. You've been warned about using language. I don't think your father can save you this time. You actually injured another child."

"He deserved it," Ryan muttered.

"That's enough! No one deserves to be hit."

"People like them do," Ryan spat, pointing his finger at Gavin, Ella, and me. "They're all freaks."

"That's enough, I said. One more word and I'm sending you home tonight."

"You can't do that!" he blurted.

Wade raised an eyebrow and said, "Watch me. I'll drive you to your parents' house myself and dump you there if I have to. You're not welcome to come back to my cabin, and they can fire me over it if they want."

Ryan's lips twisted but he said nothing.

It was satisfying, but it was bad that it had to come to this. I was glad no one was seriously hurt. I was glad I'd been able to intervene. And this was more action taken against a bully than I'd ever seen before, which gave me some hope.

Wade stood and asked the nurse, "Can Ryan stay here tonight? I know that you have a cot."

She nodded but looked like he'd asked her to suck on lemons.

"The rest of you, let's go."

Ryan's friends stood as though unsure they'd be able to go, too. When Wade didn't protest, they hurried out ahead of us all. Ella, Gavin, and I followed. Wade said a few whispered words to Ryan, whose expression darkened further, and then left. Angela came out last with the nurse's spare flashlight.

Back up the mountain we went, the two flashlights bobbing up and down with the counselors' steps. They hushed us whenever we tried to talk, so I wasn't able to say anything to Gavin or Ella, or talk to them about what had happened.

We all went back to the cabins. I was given permission to use the bathroom since I still needed to, and I hurried and dressed for bed there, too, because I didn't want anyone staring at me right then.

It took a long time to fall asleep due to all the emotions running through me.

I couldn't help but think about why Ryan had tried to beat up Gavin. If they were still friends, would Ryan have done that? If they'd been planning on beating me up, would Ryan take it out on Gavin when he was denied? Would Gavin have stood up to Ryan if he'd said something else bad about me or about gay people?

The evidence was mounting in Gavin's favor about him telling the truth about turning Ryan in, and I hadn't given him the chance. Even Ella had believed it.

But I hadn't wanted to. Guilt washed over me, and then anger. But what if it had all been staged? What if Gavin knew I'd go to the bathroom before bed, since I'd been doing just that while I'd been at camp?

Of course, I hadn't been doing that since everyone found out I was trans.

The thoughts went around and around in my head, like a hamster stuck on a wheel. Did I believe Gavin or not? Was he friends with Ryan or not? Was it staged or not? Would he go to such lengths to humiliate me, or was that a massive case of ego on my part?

I didn't want to do this to myself—didn't want to get involved. I hadn't come for romance. I'd told myself this repeatedly.

And I didn't want to hurt Gavin, not anymore. It was obvious he was as much a victim of Ryan's bullying and bigotry as I was, perhaps more so because he'd stayed friends with him for so long. I couldn't really blame him if he was as lonely and closeted as he seemed.

But I also didn't want to get involved. He'd have to hide me from his parents. He wasn't out, and I certainly wasn't going to play girl to make him feel better. Even though he hadn't asked, that was the fear I had with dating a closeted boy. Would he want me to pretend to be a girl? Was it because he, deep down, thought I was a girl or because he just wanted to use me as a way to hide his sexuality? Neither option was acceptable.

I was still mad at him, too, for his part in Ryan's plans. Maybe he'd intended to report him, maybe not. But he had remained friends with an abuser, long after he should have dumped him. Then again, Gavin himself was a victim of that abuse, and I knew how hard it was to dump the only friends you have. To leave an abusive relationship was hard. My mom was the prime example. But it could be done, and it never was the fault of the victim. It was unfair to blame Gavin, even partially.

I had to talk to Gavin. I had to hear his side of it. Once I decided that, I was able to sleep.

Chapter Eight

THE NEXT DAY was somber in the cabin. Half of the kids resented Gavin and me for our role in Ryan's exile, though it wasn't our fault. Though they'd been involved in the fight, their parents hadn't been called. They'd still received punishment, though, and now had to clean the whole cabin themselves, with Wade glaring at them the entire time. Gavin looked as though someone had just taken away his favorite puppy. His parents had come and gone early in the morning, and I was torn over whether I was relieved or annoyed that he was still there.

Alex was the only one who was speaking to me.

"What's up with everyone?" he asked as we left the cabin. We were now exempt from chores, so we decided to hang out at one of the lodges until it was time to go down for breakfast.

"You didn't hear the drama last night, did you?" I asked.

"Not really. I know that Wade left, and that he ordered us to stay inside. But I was so tired I fell asleep soon after."

I told him about discovering Ryan about to beat up Gavin. "Everyone else is mad at us for turning Ryan in."

Alex made a sound of disgust. "That's stupid. But...Gavin was telling the truth?" He gave me a sly look.

"Are you shipping us together?" I asked, a little annoyed.

Alex giggled, a sound I hadn't heard from him before.

"What is up with you and Ella? Have you two been talking behind my back?" I asked.

The smile fell from Alex's face, but he didn't look away like he'd have done before. "In all honesty? I had a crush on you, Casey."

My jaw dropped. "W-what?"

Alex waved a hand. "Don't worry about it. I got over it."

"Uh...okay?"

"I really, really liked you when we first got here. I mean, I could barely talk to you, remember?"

"Heh, I thought you hated me because you wouldn't talk to me."

He shrugged self-consciously. "I'm shy. But, once I got to know you, the crush kind of...settled into friendship. Does that make sense? I guess I really just wanted to be your friend."

"Okay. Um...thanks, I think?"

"Oh, no, no, it's not because you're not attractive. You are. It's just that I think we wouldn't go well together except as friends."

"Uh, thanks." I was at a loss for words, but after a moment, I added, "I guess I was so clueless about it. I...I was too focused on Gavin to notice anyone else."

"It's okay. I wasn't sure about you anyway. I wasn't sure if you were gay or not."

"Bi, actually, but yeah."

We moved on to talking about how great it was that we weren't cleaning anymore, and a little bit of smugness over Ryan's friends having to make our beds for us.

"I hope they don't leave anything in it," Alex said, and we laughed. I wouldn't put it past them to do something like that.

He turned serious then. "Hey, I'm sorry for the part I played in this."

"What do you mean?"

"Well, I heard Ryan talking about you, making fun of you. Gavin was there, but I didn't hear him say anything. I told you that to break you guys up."

While that was a shitty thing to do, I kind of understood. "No, it's okay." A tiny bit of anger flared in my chest, but I smothered it. Alex may have had an ulterior motive for telling me about Gavin and Ryan, but it'd been a good thing. It'd shown Gavin what a jerk Ryan was. While that hadn't been great for Gavin, it was probably for the best in the end. One part of me was happy Alex had confessed because it meant Gavin wasn't the jerk I thought he was.

I firmly told that part of myself to shut up.

Everyone had started to line up for breakfast, so we joined the crowd. They were all chattering a little louder than usual, and a few times, I caught my name or Ryan's. Word was getting around as to what had happened last night.

Gavin was standing by himself, hunched over with his arms folded over his chest. I didn't know what to say to him, so I didn't say anything—just walked down the mountain with Alex. While I needed to talk to Gavin, I didn't know how to do it. I didn't know how to start.

Ella, Nick, and Lily joined us at breakfast, and, of course, we got interrogated over what had happened. Ella kept silent, not wanting to talk about what her part had been. She played ignorant to the whole thing.

I could see other campers craning their necks, looking at us and around the room for the missing campers. But Ryan wasn't there. It didn't seem like he was going to come back.

I also managed to notice Gavin wasn't there, either. I wondered what had happened to him. Why would he miss breakfast?

But halfway through, the nurse brought him in, whispering to Wade. Gavin found a seat far away from everyone and half-heartedly started pulling food toward his plate. His eyes were red.

When I turned back to my own food, I noticed Ella's eyes on me. They were intense, shining and hard, and her mouth was pressed into a line.

"What?" I asked.

She leaned forward and whispered at me, her words cutting like glass, "After all that, you're going to ignore him? Didn't all this prove you're wrong about him?"

"It hasn't proven anything," I said, but I didn't really believe it myself.

I noticed Alex scowling at me, too, and felt betrayed.

"How could you say that? His friend was going to beat him up. He had to be telling the truth. He sang that song for you," Ella said.

"That doesn't mean he wasn't a jerk."

"But it proves he was telling the truth to you."

"No it doesn't," I insisted.

Ella made a noise of disgust and turned away. Alex didn't look happy, either, and he didn't say much to me the rest of the meal.

I knew she was right. I just didn't want to admit I was wrong. Despite what Alex had told me, I still had doubts about Gavin. And I still didn't want a romance. We only had two days left of camp. I didn't want to start something that was going to go nowhere.

I told her all of those reasons, but I could tell she wasn't listening. She had her mind set on getting us together, and there was nothing I could do to persuade her otherwise. Normally, I found her need to get her friends together charming and cute, but now it was just annoying.

We finished breakfast and returned up the mountain to sign up for morning activities. But before I could ask what they were interested in, both Ella and Alex had disappeared. So I signed up for Frisbee and didn't worry about it. I lingered at the tables for a bit, but when they never showed up, I went back down to the field for my activity.

Neither one showed up for it, though, and I felt a little bad. Had I really angered Ella and Alex that much?

I lost interest in the game after that thought, so I bowed out and went to lie in the grass instead. The sky was bright blue, speckled with fluffy white clouds. It was another beautiful day.

Only two more days of camp.

Part of me couldn't wait to go home. The other part never wanted it to end. I wanted Ella to go back to normal, not trying to fix me up with Gavin so desperately. She sometimes did this at home, but this felt different. She wanted it too much.

And me? She wanted it so bad, so I resisted it. The more she pushed, the more I would resist. It had happened before, but she'd usually relented. Did she like Gavin that much? She barely knew him—neither of us knew him that well.

But if we had more time...

No. I stopped that thought. I didn't want to get involved. Not now. Not with Gavin. I wasn't going to be his "girlfriend," though I had no evidence he thought that was what I would be. He'd never said anything to make me think that, but there it was. It was something that put a distance between me and any boy I might date.

The game had petered out around me, and I heard the others making their way back up the mountain. I decided to follow and see if I couldn't find Ella or Alex. I wanted to talk to them about this.

But I couldn't find them. No one seemed to know where they'd gone to, either. Should I worry about them? Should I tell Wade?

I went back to my bunk and tried to read for a while, but I couldn't concentrate. Where was everyone? The other boys in the cabin were avoiding me, and no one else could be found.

Strange.

I ended up staring at nothing until lunchtime, fuming and worrying alternating. And I wouldn't have even noticed it was time except I could see the crowd forming from the window next to my bunk. I jumped off my bed and rushed to line up.

Wade was there, and so were Alex and Gavin.

I went up to Alex. "Hey, what's up?"

He shrugged. "Nothing. Ready for lunch?"

"Where were you guys? I went and played Frisbee, but you weren't there."

"Nah, wanted to do something else."

"What did you do?"

But he avoided the question by walking away, following the crowd down toward the dining hall.

Annoyed, I followed. We all got seats together again, as usual, but Ella and Alex kept deftly sidestepping my questions, breezily answering only each other.

"Okay, fine," I said, finally angry. "I'll go sit somewhere else."

I grabbed my plate and, despite their sudden protests, moved across the hall and sat at one of the emptier tables. Being all alone made lunch miserable, but I wasn't going to sit with them while they ignored my questions. Something was up, and I was pretty sure I knew what it was. Ella was acting too smug, and I noticed Gavin didn't look quite so upset anymore.

That made me angrier, and I stopped eating. I sat there through the rest of the meal, feeling betrayed and furious. Why couldn't she respect my wishes and leave me out of her matchmaking? Why couldn't she set Alex up instead?

They announced the Clean Cabin Award—Cabin Two, so not us again—and then asked for volunteers for a special event that night for Canteen. After thinking about it, I wondered if they'd just let me sit everything else out for the rest of the day. I didn't want to be around anyone, not even the counselors. Wade also mentioned that Alex and I, since we'd won the talent show, could have a pizza party and invite a friend each. That was great, but I really didn't care. Maybe I'd send Ella and Gavin together instead of me, so they could keep scheming.

I was one of the first out of the door when they dismissed us, not waiting for Ella or Alex, and stormed up the mountain and went straight for the cabin without talking to anyone.

Since I was the first there, I stripped and got into bed, eagerly using the excuse of Quiet Time to not speak to anyone.

Too angry to sleep, I used the time to calm down a little bit. The other boys came into the cabin and settled down while I stared out the windows, my back to them all, including Gavin. I had heard his voice but didn't want to see him. The bed shook as he climbed into his bed underneath me, though.

I couldn't believe Ella was being like this. What was up with her?

After Quiet Time, I asked Wade if I could stay in the cabin for afternoon activities.

"No," he said. "You need to go and do something. There's only two more days left!"

"Please? I just want to read." I almost lied and told him I wasn't feeling well, but I didn't want a trip down to the nurse.

"No. Now go sign up for something."

Heaving a sigh, I went to Lincoln Lodge and looked over what they had for activities. The signup sheets were mostly full, but there were a couple open ones with no limit. One of them was called I'll Make You Laugh. Intrigued, I signed up for that one. It was meeting at the field, but in the smaller area beside the pavilion instead of the main field, where Capture the Flag would be.

I stomped back down the mountain and across the field next to the pavilion.

No surprise, Lars was the counselor for this activity. That day, he was dressed in a golden-yellow frock with tiny pink flowers, but he was wearing denim bell-bottoms underneath. He'd pulled his hair up into a little bun and ringed it with real flowers picked from the forest behind us.

"Okay, everyone," he said once it looked like we had all the campers present. "Who has played this before?"

A handful of people raised their hands. "Okay, great." He pointed to one of them. "You're going to be 'it' to start us off."

He got us to form a circle, and then we sat down. The person who was "it" had to find someone and try to make them laugh. They couldn't touch the person, but anything else was game. After the attempt, the person had to say, with a straight face, "Darling, I love you, but I just won't laugh." If you did laugh, you became "it," too.

It was a ridiculous game, and I almost got up to leave right then and there. I didn't want someone trying to make me laugh, and I kicked myself for signing up for this in the first place. What had I been thinking?

But I stayed anyway. What else could I do? I didn't want to join Capture the Flag or the Greek dodgeball game, either. Everything else was full and would have started already. I was stuck.

We started, and mostly, it was just watching others play the game. No one had tried me, and I wondered if my scowl was keeping them away. *Good.*

One girl did try to make funny faces at me, but they weren't all that great. Soon, there were many campers wandering the circle, trying to get us holdouts to laugh.

Eventually, there were two of us, with a crowd around each of us. It actually became more annoying, because everyone was talking at once, or trying things that had been done before. It was easy to just keep repeating, "Darling I love you, but I just won't laugh," at every attempt.

Lars called the game, declaring two of us—me and a girl I didn't know at all—the winners.

It didn't feel like winning.

By dinner, I was feeling so down I went ahead and invited Ella to the pizza party anyway. Alex had invited someone else, but I didn't pay attention much to who it was. It was sad and awkward and not at all enjoyable. I ate the pizza but didn't have any fun. Ella and Alex were polite to me, but I could tell Ella was upset with me, too. That was okay. It was better than what they were doing before, ignoring my questions and acting as though they were keeping me out of some joke.

After dinner was the mysterious activity the counselors had been cooking up. They took us all to the Lincoln Lodge, which had all the benches pushed back against the walls. We sat, some of us on the benches, some on the floor, and waited for whatever it was they were going to do.

Ella and Alex chatted at my feet while I sat on the bench, trying not to be angry. Ella kept turning to include me in the conversation, but I could see her heart wasn't into being friendly. I could relate and wondered why she didn't give it up.

Just as the counselors were about to do whatever it was, Wade cut through the crowd and tapped me on the shoulder.

"What?" I asked.

"Come with me."

Had I done something wrong? Glancing around to see everyone staring at me, I hunched over, got up, and trailed behind Wade as he led me out of Lincoln Lodge. "What's wrong?" I asked, trotting to keep up.

"Nothing, just follow me."

"Okay." Everyone was acting weird, and it was getting on my nerves.

We were heading toward the cabins, walking slowly, though, and a few times I had to stop to wait for Wade, since I didn't know where we were going. And then we passed our own cabin without stopping. Wade walked right by it and toward another...

"Um," I said.

But my counselor never stopped until, sure enough, we arrived at the deserted and off-limits cabin one. I stared at the door, not understanding.

"Why are we here?"

Wade just smiled, knocked, and said, "See for yourself."

"Ooookay."

I pulled the door open and was greeted by a huge shout of, "Surprise!"

As I stood stunned in the doorway, I realized a bunch of people had crowded into the cabin, and it had been decorated.

Instead of the bare, dusty room where Alex and I had practiced our duet, it was now clean and shining. Tiny, twinkling white lights had been strung around the cabin, and the regular light bulb had been covered with a red cloth so the glow inside was warm but dim.

In the center of the cabin was Gavin, grinning, his hands clasped before him like he was praying or hoping for something.

Somehow, Alex and Ella had beaten us to the cabin, and they were there, jumping up and down with barely contained excitement.

"What is this?" I asked, still not having stepped fully into the cabin.

"Go in and find out," Wade said, gently nudging me from behind.

I looked at him. He was smiling, too, plainly pleased with himself and everyone else.

I didn't want this. I suspected what this was, and it was embarrassing.

He tilted his head at me, questioning. I wanted to tell Wade to take me back to the lodge right now, but I couldn't bring myself to do it. Against my better judgment, I stepped into the cabin.

Gavin's eyes were locked on me, and they shone with hope.

As I neared, he stepped forward and took my hands. I let him, though I really wanted to pull away.

He tried to speak a couple of times, and I just stared at him, wishing this would be over. I wasn't going to make it easy for him, and I felt bad that he'd made this so public. I could feel everyone's eyes on us, waiting and expecting.

"I know things haven't been so great between us," Gavin finally said, "and I know that's just from a misunderstanding.

But...I was hoping that you would give me a second chance and go with me to the dance tomorrow night. Please say yes? Please be my date?" He said the last in a rush as if the quicker he said it, the more likely I was to agree.

I deflated. This is what I'd been afraid of when I opened the door. I knew what my answer had to be, and I knew it wasn't what he wanted. I glanced around and met Ella's gaze. She mouthed *Say yes* to me. I looked away.

"I...Gavin. I..."

I couldn't go on. I didn't want to hurt him, but I couldn't say yes. There was so much we had to work out before then. I had to be sure he hadn't been involved in Ryan's plot. And I couldn't be with someone who would just abuse me later. I needed to protect myself, to make sure he wasn't dating me so he could pretend I was a girl while he was straight to his parents. I wasn't going to do that.

Gavin said, "Please leave us alone." His voice was only just above a whisper.

"Gavin, no..."

But everyone left. Before she went, Ella pinched me and pulled me to the side. "Don't break his heart,"

"What about me?"

"You know what I think."

I didn't have anything to say to that, so I closed my mouth with a snap.

They left Gavin and me alone in the darkness, lit only by the twinkling lights and the dim red light from above.

"I'm sorry, Gavin," I said. "I didn't want that to be so public."

"No, it's okay. I...I should have known how this would go."

"Then why did you do it?"

"Because I wanted you to give me a chance. This was the only way I thought I could get you alone."

"By having my friends lie to me, by deceiving me?"

He blanched. "It wasn't a lie. It was a surprise."

I snorted. "Not much difference."

"Casey, you're not making this easy."

"Good, I shouldn't be."

He turned away, holding himself, and paced the small space in the cabin. "I just want to know why you said no."

"Isn't it obvious?"

"Don't play that with me. Have the courage to say it."

It was my turn to blanch. "Okay. Because I still think you and Ryan were planning something. That you were going to allow him to beat me up so you could stay closeted to your parents. He had that over you, did he?"

"He still does. My parents don't know."

"And that's another problem. I'm not going to date you, and then have you make me play girl for your parents."

"What?" The shock in his voice was so genuine it took me aback.

But I went on. "I'm not going to hide, either. Look, Gavin, I know what it's like to be closeted." I stopped short, my mouth hanging open, realizing with a start what a hypocrite I'd been. I sighed, and the welling anger inside me deflated like a pierced balloon. "You know, my parents don't know I'm bi. I mean, they know about the trans stuff, but I think they've only ever thought I'd bring home girls. I haven't told them I was bi because I thought it would be too much at once."

"My parents would probably kill me," Gavin muttered. "They're not okay with gay people."

"That's terrible."

"It's why I've hidden it. But...I can't do it anymore. Not now." He put his head in his hands. I wanted to reach out and touch him, console him, but I couldn't. He'd take it the wrong way.

"What will you do?"

"I don't know. But...I never once thought of you as a girl. I honestly didn't know until I saw you that time at the pool. I would never, ever do that to you. I want you to know that."

"Thank you," I said and meant it. He'd never done anything to warrant me thinking he would...but the fear was always there. It might be unfair to think it of him, but I still had to protect myself.

"I do want to tell my parents." He sank onto the cabin floor and ran a finger over the rough wood. "I just don't know how."

I sat next to him, but not close enough to touch. I didn't want that temptation. "Do you think they'll do something bad?"

"Yeah. Maybe. I don't know. Really? I don't know. I think maybe it'll depend on how I do it. That's kind of why I thought I'd be able to hide it, you know, until I went away for school or something."

"That's a long time." I thought about how long I was going to have to wait to start testosterone and get top surgery. It felt like an eternity.

"I know. And I don't think I can do it anymore. I don't want to date girls, even to stay in the closet. I just don't think I can fake it. There's so much pressure to date, though."

"I know what you mean." It had become impossible to keep my being trans to myself any longer than I had. I might have exploded had I stayed a girl in everyone else's eyes.

"I'm sure you do. So...what did you do when you told your parents you're trans?"

I smiled at the memory. "I just told them. Just...one night at dinner I blurted it out. Surprised them both, but it was good to get it off my chest. I told them I needed to dress like a boy, act like a boy, be treated like a boy, be a boy, or I didn't know how long I could be alive."

"Wow, that's...scary."

"Well, it was true. I was so miserable I couldn't stand it. I hated dressing like a girl, being treated like a girl. It just wasn't me. I needed them to understand that."

He stared at the floor for a minute, and we fell into an uncomfortable silence. Then, "I'm sorry I embarrassed you."

"No, it's okay." I don't know why I did it, but I reached out and grabbed his arm, giving it a squeeze. He looked at me in surprise and then smiled shyly at me. His eyes shone in the dim light. "I'm glad we got to talk. It's made me feel a lot better. Has it helped you?"

He licked his lips. "Yeah, it has."

"Good."

"I still wish you'd go to the dance with me."

I took my hand away. "I know. I'm not ready for dating much yet, okay?"

"I think I understand. You're not ready to tell your parents you're bi, either, right?"

He had me there. "Yeah, I think so. Look, I know I haven't been nice about it. It's just, really, there's only a little more than a day left..."

There was a strong knock on the door, and then it slammed violently open. It rattled in the hinges, bounced off the wall, and shuddered to a halt, still open. We both jumped, spinning to see who had barged in. It was Wade, eyeing us.

"Just checking nothing funny was going on in here," he said, his voice booming in the room.

Gavin and I shared a look and then laughed.

"No," I said, "nothing funny at all."

"That's good." Wade looked around again, as though searching for evidence we'd been doing something we shouldn't have. "You two have been alone long enough. Come on, come out and join everyone else."

Gavin and I got up and left the cabin. I wanted to talk to him more, tell him my reasoning behind why I didn't want to get involved. To ask him about Ryan and why they'd stayed friends for so long. But it all seemed so stupid now. Flimsy excuses. I'd been hiding behind hypocrisy, not realizing the reason I hadn't wanted to date him was because I was afraid of what my parents would think, too. I hadn't even acknowledged it to myself, hiding behind Gavin's own closeted status and using that as an excuse.

Wade led us all back to Lincoln. Screams and laughter boiled out of the lodge, and I wondered what was going on. We went in and found Lars and a bunch of the other counselors dressed in the most ridiculous costumes, rolling all over the floor. Behind them, a banner hung from the rafters, which read: "Gross, Grosser, and GROSSEST!"

They were finishing up whatever it was. I asked a kid sitting nearby what was going on, and she said, "A game show!" in between peals of laughter.

Lars had put some sort of makeup on so he looked like he'd half peeled his skin off, and he was rolling around in what I could only imagine was watered-down oats and peanut butter. It looked worse than that. He also wore a pink tutu, a red bonnet, and a sleeveless T-shirt stained with...something.

He stood up, his arms up over his head, and everyone cheered. Stuck in his armpit hair was more of the oat and peanut butter mixture. It definitely was disgusting. I joined in the cheering, but I barely knew what was going on.

The other counselors lined up, and Angela, who looked a little green even under her dark skin, said, "Okay, everyone, time to vote! Who was the most disgusting?"

Lars clearly won that one. He was still spitting up oats and peanut butter, and some of it even came out of his nose right as everyone was clapping to vote for him. There were groans, and the cheering increased.

I hadn't noticed them before, but two campers who had been standing behind Lars ran up and hugged him as Angela pronounced him the winner. They were dressed in identical tutus and bonnets. Angela said, "And his two helpers, Mia and Ibrahim, have also won! Congratulations, everyone. You two are exempt from cabin cleaning duties for the last day!"

It wasn't much of a prize, but it was something.

I hadn't noticed it, but Gavin's arm was resting on my leg. It seemed casual, like I just happened to be there when he leaned over and needed support for his arm. But he was holding himself stiffly, as though he couldn't believe I was letting him touch me.

He detected me finally noticing it, but he didn't move, only stayed carefully still. I was shocked I hadn't noticed it before then. In my defense, I'd been entranced by Lars rolling around in fake vomit.

And now that I knew his arm was there, I realized I kind of liked it.

But I couldn't do this. I stood up, and he yanked his arm back. He didn't look at me, playing it off as though he was just politely letting me up.

I hurried to the showers, trying not to think. At least Ryan wasn't there to bug me, and it made me happier that the last couple of days would be bully-free for both Gavin and me.

The whole time I was under the showerhead, I could still feel the pressure of Gavin's arm on my leg.

So much had happened that day I thought I'd have a hard time falling asleep. But I was so tired I drifted off easily. I dreamed of Gavin in ways that were embarrassing to remember.

Chapter Nine

THE NEXT MORNING at breakfast, Ella wasn't speaking to me.

"Come on, Ella," I pleaded. "We made up, but I'm just not going to date him, okay?"

But she huffed and didn't say anything. Alex shrugged and went back to eating pancakes.

"Ella, come on, this is stupid."

She turned a withering glare on me.

"Don't know why you're so set on this." I shoveled pancake into my mouth.

By the end of breakfast, she had relaxed, though I could see tears in her eyes. "Why are you so interested in getting us together?" I asked her.

She turned a watery smile on me. "I just want you to be happy. And I thought you two looked so cute together."

"Is that it?"

"I just felt so bad for him. He's never dated."

I hadn't really, either, not for real. "Same."

"I know. That's why it would be so perfect for you two."

"Well, it's a nice thought, but it's not going to happen."

Alex chimed in, "You did look cute together. I was super jealous."

We all chuckled, even me, and I was glad Alex had relaxed enough to be friends with us. I still felt bad for not even noticing his crush. I knew friendship was no substitute, but I took him at his word. He just wanted to be friends now.

Everyone was so excited about the dance that night no one could concentrate on anything else. Apparently the counselors knew this, and all the activities for the morning were physical ones requiring lots of running. Lunch came and went, and all of a sudden, it was time for dinner and getting ready for the dance.

Ella had already agreed, of course, to be my "date."

I didn't really have much for the dance in terms of nice clothes, so I borrowed a shirt from Gavin and wore my nice jeans again.

The shirt smelled like Gavin, even though it was clean. He smelled of soap and fresh air, and it made me happy when I pulled it over my head.

The counselors had gone all out for the dance, which would be at the pavilion. But that wasn't the only thing they had decorated. White Christmas lights had been strung on the trees all along the road as far as the cords could reach. Where the lights ended, they'd started a line of those little flickering electric votive "candles." Everything twinkled brightly in the darkness, like fairies among the trees.

Ella met me just at the start of the votives, wearing a blue sundress that made her look even paler than usual. Her honey-colored hair was down, curling in waves around her face and shoulders. I gave her a peck on the cheek, which caused her to blush. "You're the only one who can do that," she admitted, and I wasn't sure if she meant making her blush or the kiss. It didn't matter.

"You look lovely," I told her, because she needed to hear it.

We held hands, swinging them back and forth, as we walked together down the mountain. She gasped at the pretty lights, excited over the romantic setting even though she didn't get much from it. She was excited for everyone else.

Alex had demurred when we asked if he wanted to come with us as friends, but we met up with him halfway down the mountain. He was holding hands with a boy I didn't know well, but I recognized him as the one Alex had invited to the pizza party. I'd been so miserable I hadn't noticed him. I slapped Alex on the shoulder in congratulations, and the other boy, Chris, looked shy but pleased.

It had all worked out well, I thought.

The pavilion was a dazzling display of lights. Someone had strung up a disco ball from the high rafters, and it threw sparkles all over the floor and out into the night. A large ancient stereo system blasted popular music that a few campers were already awkwardly dancing to. More Christmas lights were strung up high on each of the support posts, topped with silver bows and white flowers.

A few couples had already given up on dancing and sat on the grass instead, intent on one another. Counselors kept an eye out, but didn't disturb anyone. There was a rule against making out, but it looked as though it was being relaxed for tonight, at least a little.

Ella and I danced for a few songs, staying close to Alex and Chris. Alex was also an amazingly skilled dancer, and he showed Chris how to do some of the popular moves. We followed along, clumsily, laughing at our poor skills until we were all sweating and tired.

I was parched after that, so I went to get Ella and me some punch. Gavin was hovering nearby, and I smiled and nodded at him. He was alone, looking rather lost.

"Hey," I called to him. "Come hang with us."

He poured himself some punch too and followed me back to where Ella, Alex, and Chris had collapsed onto the grass. Nick and Lily, with their dates, also joined us. I wasn't at all surprised that Lily was clutching another girl's hand, but Nick had asked a pretty girl to be his date. I didn't know either of them.

I sank down next to Ella, and we made room for Gavin so we were all in a big circle. Ella was eyeing me significantly, but I decided to ignore her.

"Having fun?" she asked Gavin as he sipped his punch.

Bobbling his head, he said, "I guess so. Kind of lonely." He didn't see the look I threw him at the barb, but turned toward her. "Ella, would you like to dance? You look beautiful."

She beamed at him, checked with me to see if it was okay, and then hurried off with him. I watched them dancing together, and Gavin was a perfect gentleman with her. She laughed at something he said, throwing her head back. I wondered if she knew how pretty she was, and I hoped she did. I told her all the time, but I wasn't sure she believed me.

Alex's date and I chatted a bit. He seemed nice enough, and Alex was fawning over him, so that worked out well. Apparently, they lived in the same city, so they'd be able to continue their relationship after camp.

A tiny band of jealousy squeezed my heart.

After a couple of songs, Gavin and Ella stumbled back to our circle, breathless. They'd just completed a Lindy Hop piece, having discovered that both of them knew enough to muddle through a song.

Gavin lay back on the grass, his arms and legs spread wide as he panted. His white shirt clung to him, and I couldn't help but notice his flat chest rising and falling.

A part of me wanted to touch him there, open his shirt and run my fingers down his chest. I bit my hand to keep from reaching out. Ella noticed and winked at me, and I knew exactly what she was trying to do.

It was, unfortunately, working.

I couldn't believe my own emotions were betraying me like this. But I couldn't stop staring at Gavin.

I shot to my feet and lurched off to get more punch, needing to get away. I couldn't do this. Not now. Not with only one night left. I might never see him again.

But what if he's worth it? What if all of this is worth it?

I stood by the punch bowl, my back turned to the dancers, and stared into my drink. The music blared, but all I could hear was the roaring in my ears. I was so hot, melting in the summer heat in my binder. My heart was pounding in my chest, and the heat of the blood in my face was as if I'd just opened an oven and stuck my head inside.

Why couldn't I just enjoy the rest of the night with Ella, dancing and having fun with friends? It was exactly what I'd wanted all along.

I was so absorbed in my thoughts I jumped when a hand snaked around my shoulder. I turned to see Gavin so close, his face only inches from mine. He was smiling gently. "Are you okay?" The music was loud, but I could hear him just fine. All my senses seemed to be straining toward him. His arm was warm on my shoulders.

"Y-yeah, I'm fine."

"Do you want to dance?"

I tried to say, "We shouldn't." But it came out, "Sure."

He took my hand and led me onto the dance floor. I think my hand started to sweat, but he didn't seem to care. He pulled me close, chest to chest. My first thought was how much I wished I wasn't wearing a binder, so I could feel what we were doing. I noticed he was only a little taller than me, and we could almost see eye to eye. I kind of liked that, though I usually didn't like being so short. It felt really intimate, being so close.

We swayed together to the music, gazing into one another's eyes. His were so blue, with flecks of white and gray. I memorized every freckle on his face, adoring every one of them. I couldn't tell what he was thinking, but he must have liked what he saw.

He leaned in close, his hair tickling my face. "Do you want to kiss me?" he whispered. I shuddered, both from what he had asked and because of his breath on my skin.

"I...I..." was all I could say.

He pulled away and looked at me, meeting my eyes again. I did want to kiss him, but I wasn't sure I wanted to do that here, now.

"Do you? I won't unless you say yes." His eyes searched my face, flicking here and there. We'd stopped dancing, but I'd barely noticed.

"I, uh, yes."

"Yes?"

"Yes."

His lips twitched in a half smile, and then he leaned in close. He smelled so good.

Our lips met, and I closed my eyes. His lips were soft and warm, and I could taste the punch on them. It was a small kiss, and he pulled away to look at me again.

"Yes?" he asked.

"Yes," I said, breathless. But I said it. I didn't want to stop.

We came together, brushing our lips at first, and then he wrapped his arms all the way around me and pulled me into a tight embrace. Gavin pressed his mouth to mine, crushing our lips together. His tongue flicked across mine, and though I'd never kissed someone like that before, I opened my mouth and let him in.

His tongue was soft, and we explored each other, hungry and dying of hunger. His hands were on my face, lifting my chin. I slid mine down to his butt and squeezed. He laughed against my lips, pulling away as his face reddened.

"Too much?" I asked.

"No, no, it's okay. Just...I've never done this before..." His breath was shaking.

"Me neither." Not with another boy, not really with anyone. I liked it a lot.

I watched the fetching blush fade from his face as we stood there on the dance floor, awkwardly not touching now. It almost seemed anticlimactic to go back to dancing. But I picked up his hands and put them back on my waist anyway. I wanted him to touch me.

"So what does this mean?" he asked.

"I don't know," I answered. "What do you want it to mean?"

He moved his arms up to my shoulders and leaned his head in so we touched foreheads. His eyes were closed. "I want this to mean something." The words were almost lost in the music. We were so close, though, that I heard him. He sounded lost, alone, and I wanted to never hear him sound like that again.

I had fallen hard for Gavin, and it was too late. There was no going back now. "Me, too"

He lifted his head and looked at me, his brow furrowed. When he saw I meant it, he kissed me again, drawing me in as close as we could get. I wanted to meld with him, sink into his flesh to get even closer to him. My chest was in the way, even through the binder, damn it.

We separated again, and he put his forehead back on mine. "I can't believe we're doing this. It's...wonderful." Was that a tear in his eye?

"Oh, Gavin, are you okay?"

"Yeah, I'm more than okay. I...just never thought I'd be with someone like you. It's great. I...I can't keep this from my parents." He sniffled a little.

"Let's go sit and talk."

He agreed, and we went hand in hand to a new patch of grass. I didn't want to look at Ella, because I knew the look of triumph that would be plastered on her face.

We sat, and Gavin laid his head in my lap so he could look up at me. I brushed the hair out of his face, and he closed his eyes, obviously enjoying the touch. My fingers traced the line of his brows, as red as his hair, and he sighed in happiness. His skin and hair were so soft and downy, like bird feathers.

"I worry about what my parents will say," he said. "I worry that they'll misgender you. Worry they'll think I'm straight, but you're weird. I want them to know exactly who I am, and who you are."

"I can handle the misgendering," I said. "I'll correct them. My parents will probably be here, too."

The plan was to ride back with Ella again, but after everything that had happened, I was pretty sure my parents would be coming. Even if they didn't, Ella's parents would set Gavin's straight.

"That would be great," he said. "But I don't want to put you through that, and I don't want us to hide. I'm ready to come out; I just don't know how to do it."

"I know." I understood completely. It was a hard thing to do, especially if he was going to be trapped in a car with them for hours. What awful things could they say to him during that time?

He reached up and took my hand, which was still touching his face. His skin was so soft. "Do you want to be my boyfriend?" he asked.

I knew what I should say. I shouldn't get too involved. What if his parents were awful to me? What if we could never see each other again? What would happen to him if I did become his boyfriend? There were so many ways this could end badly. It was already starting out badly, at the end of two weeks of camp. This was the last night. While we could always exchange our information and keep in contact through social media and our phones, it would be a long-distance relationship.

I'd barely had any relationships at all. Did I want to put the effort into keeping up a long distance one? Would my parents be willing to help me out and drive us to meet one another sometimes? Wouldn't my time be better spent on relationships with boys (or girls) near me, in my own state?

Gavin sat up. I'd hesitated too long. "I understand," he said, and his tone was dead. He started to stand up, but I stopped him, taking his hand before he could go too far.

"No, don't go. I...I'm just not sure. I do want to be your boyfriend, I do. But...how will we make it work? Have you ever done a long-distance relationship?"

"No," he admitted. "I haven't done any sort of relationship. But I'd be willing to try. For you."

"For me?"

His look was anguished. "Yes, for you."

I swallowed hard. Could I do this? Did I want to do this?

Should I give in? It meant a lot of changes for me. I'd have to tell my parents I was bi, though that was minor I supposed, compared to everything else.

He sat back down, his eyes once more searching my face for my answer. I reached out and touched his lips. What if I couldn't ever touch him again? See him again? What if his parents forbade us?

The words stuck in my throat. I couldn't say them, couldn't crush him, but I couldn't say yes, either. I wanted to do both, in equal measures. I'd fallen hard and fast and didn't have the time to sort out my emotions. This wasn't the place to do this, with him so close.

I felt horrible, crushed inside, like I had killed something inside me. The intensity of the feeling frightened me, and it choked off any words that I could say. There were so many things I wanted to tell Gavin, but they all jammed together, blocking the flow and preventing anything from getting out.

"I understand." He pulled away and stood once more, his eyes sad. But he held out his hand to me and helped me up. "Dance with me again anyway?"

"Yes," I said. That I could do.

The song was a fast one, but that didn't matter. He put aside his sadness and showed me a few steps to fit the song. I tried, stumbling over my feet and stepping on his a few times. It lightened the mood, and soon we were laughing again. My heart lifted to see him so happy.

That song ended, and a slow one began. The dance floor, which had previously been mostly empty, filled again. Couples danced all around us. Gavin drew me closer to him. He still smelled good, even though both of us were sweating. I wanted to bury my face in his hair. Instead, I ran my fingers through it, and he closed his eyes in pleasure.

"Don't do this to me," he whispered against my lips. "Please, please tell me you will say yes. Please say yes."

I curled up close to him, resting my head on his chest. I had to hunch a little bit, but I liked being there. Even through the music, I could hear and feel his heart beating.

I couldn't say no.

I couldn't say yes.

The feelings warred within me, tearing me apart. But finally, I could stay silent no longer.

I looked up at him, into those blue eyes, and said, "Yes. Yes, I'll be your boyfriend." It felt reckless, throwing my fate into the wind. It didn't matter that this might end horribly. I needed to try it.

The joy on his face was worth it. He crushed me in a hug, picking me up and swinging me around. A laugh burst from me, and we nearly tumbled over. He was strong, but not that much bigger than me. We caught our balance on each other, and then we were kissing again.

Those kisses were hard and desperate, but joyful, too, and I let them happen. I wanted us both to be happy, and while I thought this was going to be hard, it was also going to be worth it.

We finished the dance and then decided we needed some food.

Hand in hand, we wandered over to the snack table and got more punch and a few things to munch on. "Do you want to go back to your friends?" Gavin asked.

"Yeah, let's tell them."

He initially looked as though he didn't really want to go, but his face brightened at the suggestion.

"I'm done hiding," I told him.

"Me, too."

We made our way to the others, who were still sprawled in the grass. Ella was sweating, but her face was radiant. Even though she didn't say anything to us, her whole body practically vibrated with joy as we joined them.

We sat with our knees touching. Alex was grinning at us. His date was off getting more food for them as well.

I wasn't sure if we should say anything, or make it casual. But I didn't want to hurt Gavin, so, I said, "Hey Ella, meet my new boyfriend."

It was a good thing I'd set down my punch, because Ella launched herself at me and squished me in a hug, almost bowling me completely over. I caught myself from falling onto my back, but just barely. She was shaking me, laughing and crying at the same time.

"You silly boy! I'm so happy for you, though! Why did it take you so long? You're hopeless!"

She finally let me go after alternating between gushing and scolding for a few minutes. I had to tell her she was pressing too hard on my already-taxed ribs. With a gasp, she let me go, nearly pushing me away. Gavin had watched, amused, until she threw herself at him, too.

"See? I told you," she said. "He's just a little dense sometimes."

"Hey," I protested, but she was right. Sometimes I was pretty dense. I thought too much and felt too little, and didn't notice those around me until they smacked me upside the head, metaphorically speaking.

Our eyes met, and Gavin winked at me over Ella's sobbing shoulder.

She finally wiped her eyes and got up only to plop down next to me. "I'm so happy for you two."

Gavin took my hand and squeezed it. "Me, too."

We danced a couple more times, but before the night was over, Ella drew me aside to walk along the edge of the field.

"I'm so glad you and Gavin are going to give it a try." She held onto my arm as we matched pace with each other.

"Me, too," I said. "Thank you for not giving up on me."

She beamed at me and then poked me hard in the ribs. "You're so hopeless sometimes."

We were quiet for a ways, and then she said what had been bothering her the whole time. She'd been trying to hide it, but I knew her too well. I hadn't wanted to say anything to ruin the night. Her bringing it up on her own was better.

"I just wanted to say thanks, for supporting me, too."

"What do you mean?"

"About me being ace." She looked up at me, her eyes serious and sparkling in the dim light from the pavilion. "It means a lot."

"I'm not perfect, you know that, but I try." I didn't tell her about all those times I wished she'd just get a boyfriend and leave me alone. It would hurt her, but she should still know that some people thought it.

"I know," she said. "I can see it on your face. You want me to be normal."

"You are normal," I said. "Just different."

"Not everyone thinks so."

"Ella—"

"No, Casey, it's okay. I think I'm finally okay with it. I know you've been pretty preoccupied with everything that's happened, but I think I finally figured it all out."

"I'm sorry I'm so self-absorbed."

She chuckled softly. "It's okay. But, yeah. I'm ace, and there's nothing wrong with that."

She hadn't framed it as a question, but I could hear it in her words.

"No, Ella, there's nothing wrong with that. You're just you. You meddle in my love life but you need none of your own. That's okay."

She pinched me. "I don't meddle."

"Sure."

She pinched me again, harder, and I yelled, "Ow!"

"You deserve it," she said.

Maybe I did.

"I'm kind of glad Ryan was here," she continued.

"What, why?"

"Because it all brought you and Gavin together. And it made me see how right I was in not giving in to dating him or anyone else."

"We might have gotten there without him. We don't need people like Ryan around to help us understand ourselves."

"Maybe not. Or maybe so," she said. "But maybe we need the darkness to see the light."

"I guess. But it sure would be nice if the dark wasn't quite so...dark...all the time."

"You're right."

We'd made the circuit around the field and come back to the pavilion and our friends. She squeezed my arm and ran off to dance again by herself, just moving to the joy of the music. I rejoined Gavin, who'd been waiting for me.

Our magical night was starting to wind down. Gavin and I got up for one last dance when it was called, and held each other close. I was glad we got to do it, and that no one cared two boys were kissing and dancing together. Ella had been right after all, about many things.

I looked out over Gavin's shoulder to see multiple couples taking their last chance at dancing together. There was Alex and Chris, and Lily and her partner (girlfriend?). Ella was dancing still, but now with Nick, whose date seemed to have wandered off. There were lots of couples, of every variety, and that made me happy. It was the way it should be, and I was frankly stunned at the acceptance. Ella had been right in that, too: I loved it here.

Finally, Lars switched the music off, and we were all instructed to go back to the cabins. Ella, Gavin, and I held hands, with me in the middle, all the way back up the mountain. My heart was full, and I barely noticed the usual trudge up the steep incline. I wasn't entirely certain my feet were touching the ground, instead of floating above it on pure happiness.

We hugged Ella goodnight and continued into our cabin, thrilled we could kiss each other goodnight, even though we couldn't take it any further than that. The temptation was there, but Wade was keeping too close a watch on us. I wasn't sure I was ready for that anyway.

I undressed, a little shy because I wasn't sure I was ready for Gavin to see all of me now, like this. He was a gentleman, though, and didn't watch me. Alex and Nick were there anyway, so nothing could have happened, but I wanted our first official time of seeing one another naked to be special. Not just undressing to go to bed. If we ever got that far. I hoped we would, but we were going to have to take this one step at a time.

We shared a sweet kiss, holding hands as long as we could, until Wade looked like he was going to say something to us.

That night's insomnia was caused by a good thing. I lay there, staring out the window into the warm night, remembering the whole evening.

I still couldn't believe it, and there was a small part of me that was unhappy about how things had turned out. What was I doing to myself?

But the rest of me glowed with the warmth of my first boyfriend. All of the reservations I'd had about Gavin were gone. He wanted to tell his parents about me, but he worried for me about being misgendered. While most would agree that his wanting to tell his parents about me was the right thing to do, I still appreciated him being worried on my behalf.

I don't know why it took me so long to believe him about the whole Ryan mess. He'd been as much a victim as me, and I felt bad for him that he'd had to tolerate Ryan's abuse for so long. It was only because he hadn't had anyone else. But now, he had me, and that was a good thing.

IT WAS A sad morning the next day. I could feel the dejection in the air as we packed our belongings back into our trunks. There wasn't a lot of scrambling, though, since we'd kept everything so clean all the time.

We also had to tidy up the cabin, sweeping everywhere, including under the beds now that the trunks were no longer there. Though Wade told Alex and me we were exempt due to our talent show win, we still chipped in. It was a chance to work with Gavin, as I held the pan while he swept the dirt into it.

All morning, we shared light touches as we got ready. Any time we walked past each other, we'd brush shoulders or hands, sharing a smile or a look or a shy glance. It was wonderful, but I could feel the tension building between us. We wouldn't be able to touch like this for much longer, and we both knew it. It was killing me inside, knowing it was the only day we had together.

We had one last meal at the dining hall, and Wade hustled us out of the cabin to line up for it. That time, they didn't care how we mingled, and Ella, Alex, Gavin, and I walked together.

"So where's Chris?" Ella asked, glancing around.

Alex shrugged. "It was just the one date. We'll see how it goes later on."

She looked disappointed for him, but he didn't seem to mind.

"I'm happy with taking it slow," he reassured her.

Gavin and I held hands, swinging them between us, and sat together, our legs touching, as we ate our last meal together.

It was a good meal—waffles again with tons of butter and syrup, watermelon, strawberries, and as much bug juice as we could drink.

At the end, Wade stood and made an announcement. "Thank you everyone for coming to camp this year. We had some ups and downs, but I think this was definitely a good session!" There was polite clapping and some cheering. "We hope to see you again next year!"

"Wait...what?" Ella asked. This was supposed to be the last year for people our age.

"Oh, yes! Good news, everyone. We are expanding our program to include high school students," Wade announced after the mutters had subsided. "You are all welcome back next year for another two weeks!"

Gavin squeezed my leg. "We should come!"

Right there, we kissed again, not caring who saw (we got a few hoots), and when we pulled apart, I said, "We will." I hoped we'd see each other before then—a whole year was a long, long time—but at least this was once place we could return to and be together.

WE WAITED FOR our parents on the field and the pavilion. Gavin and I tried to sneak away for a make-out session, but we couldn't get far. Wade was making the rounds, checking up on all his charges until their parents came to collect them. He caught us and chased us out of the woods with some stern words and a threat to tell our parents. We reluctantly stayed in sight after that.

I could tell Gavin was nervous, though. He started to shake when he pointed out his parents' car. "There they are." He rubbed my knuckles with one hand while nearly crushing it in the other. "Are you ready?"

"Yes," I said. "Are you?"

"Honestly? No. But I'm going to do it anyway."

I had dressed in my most obviously boyish clothes, wishing I could have a quick haircut since mine had gotten a little shaggy. My binder was one of the newer ones I'd brought, crushing my chest completely flat. Hopefully, it would be enough for his parents to read me as a boy, and not just a boyish girl. It was important to Gavin. He wanted them to know I was a boy.

He squeezed my hand twice and then set off in his parents' direction, with me in tow.

"Do you want me to come later?" I asked as we walked.

"No. They're going to see me now."

"Okay." I admired him a little for the bravery. So many people told gay and trans people we were brave for coming out, and we were. But it was the kind of bravery that shouldn't deserve praise. We shouldn't need to be brave to tell our families our true selves. We shouldn't need to face our families with fear in our hearts. There should be no shame, no fear of rejection, for living our truth.

But there was.

His parents were older than mine, or at least his mother had let her hair go all the way to a shocking white. She had a pinched mouth that made her look even older. His dad, though, was younger-looking, but was a big man with a loud voice. I could hear him practically shouting at his wife as we neared.

"Ah, Gavin!" he boomed, holding his arms out for a hug from his son.

But Gavin stopped a few steps away, his body braced as though he was expecting a punch. Maybe he was, and that made me both sad and angry.

"Mom," he said, nodding to her. "Dad. I have someone I want you to meet."

They blinked at me, looking down and noticing our hands still linked together.

"Who is this?" his dad asked.

"This is my boyfriend." Gavin's voice did not shake, but there was a tone of defiance in it. I was holding my breath, waiting for the inevitable explosion. His hand was hot in mine, wet with fear sweat, but I didn't care.

Silence.

It stretched uncomfortably.

And then, "Don't be ridiculous, Gavin," his mother said. "Come along, we need to get your things."

"No," Gavin said. "I don't think you understand." He held up our hands, still joined and shook them a little. "I'm gay. Do you get it? This is my boyfriend."

Her face went pale, and that was saying something since she was already so fair. His dad though, reddened until he looked something like a tomato, and he blurted out, "Not here, Gavin, not here. Let's talk about this later." He looked around furtively, as though terrified of being overheard. I had to resist the urge to shout at him about how queer we were.

"No," Gavin said, breathlessly. "We'll talk about it here. You haven't said hello to Casey."

It was like a standoff. Gavin and me on one side, his parents on the other, neither speaking, neither giving ground.

"Gavin," I said, seeing Ella's parents driving up. And mine, too, as I recognized our van.

"No, Casey. They're going to have to deal with it now."

I was starting to be uncomfortable, but I knew what Gavin was going through. I would stay by him.

My parents parked next to Ella's. I needed to have my coming-out moment with them, too. I almost wished they'd walk over, so they'd be around in case Gavin's parents had a meltdown.

His mother started to fidget, looking everywhere but at us. But his dad deflated. "Is this really what you want?" he asked in a resigned tone.

Gavin relaxed a tiny bit. "Yes. Casey is my boyfriend. I'm gay. So I won't be dating any girls. Ever." He put a heavy stress on the last word, as though daring them to think I was anything other than a boy.

His mother looked like she'd swallowed a lemon whole, tasting it all the way down. But finally, she faced me and said stiffly, "It's nice to meet you, Casey." She didn't really sound like she meant it, but Gavin let out a breath next to me. I felt him release all his anxiety. He stopped squeezing my hand so hard, and I could feel my fingers again.

"Thank you, Mom," he said.

His dad nodded to me but couldn't bring himself to say anything.

Gavin nodded at them both and said, "I'm going to go say goodbye to Casey."

They looked both worried and relieved.

"Mine next," I breathed, seeing my parents looking this way and that, trying to spot me among all the other cars and campers.

My mom caught sight of me and waved, and I waved back. "We can do this," I said.

"Yours should be easy, right?" Gavin asked, putting his arm around me.

"Maybe. My dad will be the holdout."

"I thought mine would be, too."

My mom pulled me into a big hug, forcing me to drop Gavin's hand. "How was it?" she asked as she finally let me go.

She noticed Gavin and smiled. I went back to him and took his hand in my own.

"Casey?"

"Hi, Mom. Dad. Um. This is Gavin. My boyfriend."

My mom only blinked and then immediately beamed at him before crushing Gavin in a hug just as confining as the one she'd given me. He even *oofed* as she pulled him close. My dad watched us, his face neutral.

"This is wonderful news, Casey," Mom said. "You didn't tell us you were gay." Her tone was carefully neutral. I knew her. She was hurt I hadn't confided in her but didn't want it to come across as disapproval.

"Well, bi, actually," I said.

"Oh, okay." And just like that, she was okay with it all.

Some of my own tension drained away, but not all of it. My dad still hadn't said anything.

He walked over to me, his hands in his pockets, looking down at me with an expression I couldn't read. Then he stuck his hand out for Gavin to shake, which he did eagerly. My dad speared Gavin with a stern eye, still gripping his hand, and said, "Keep my son safe, okay?"

Before I knew it, tears were spilling down my cheeks.

He had called me son.

Arms were around me as I collapsed into sobs, and I didn't know whose they were. But there were many, and when I finally got control over myself, I saw we'd been in a huge group hug. When my parents let me go, Gavin kept his arm around me.

My dad gripped my shoulders in his hands. "I'm just glad you're safe," he said. "I'm glad you're my son. I'm glad you're still here." His voice was gruff from holding back the tears I could see threatening to spill down his cheeks. Mom had started to cry and was hugging him from the side.

"Thanks, Dad," I said. "I'm glad I'm your son."

His lips trembled as he pulled me into another hug.

Ella was behind us, bouncing up and down in excitement, her parents grinning behind her.

We all stepped away from one another and awkwardly introduced ourselves around. Gavin's parents had come over, cautiously, to shake hands and exchange phone numbers.

During the hubbub, Gavin was able to pull me off to one side. Now the session was over, we got out our phones and hoped we had enough charge left in them to swap numbers and profiles.

Once that was done, he drew me into another kiss. "I'm going to miss you."

"Me, too. I'm sorry we didn't have more time. That was my fault."

"No apology needed. I should have stood up to Ryan long before I even got here. I'm sorry for what almost happened to you. I'm sorry for not defending you from Ryan, for letting it get so far."

"I understand," I said, reassuring him. Ryan's plan had never happened, and that was what mattered. I hadn't yet been beaten up for being trans, but I'd been teased and threatened. I was kind of used to it, though that was a sad thought.

We kissed again, pressing our lips together for as long as we could before we had to breathe. His hands were all over my back, not even hesitating over the binder's edges. Finally, his arms went around my waist, and he picked me up as we kissed. I squealed a little in fear as I felt him waver, and we collapsed onto the soft grass in an undignified heap, laughing.

I was the first to recover, and I sat on him, my legs on either side of his chest. We paused, realizing what sort of position we were in. There was a shy moment, and then we were kissing again, his hands on my butt, mine on his face.

"Casey!" came my mom's call, and we hastily pulled apart. I helped him stand, and we went back to join our parents.

Mom was eyeing me, but I knew it wasn't because I was with Gavin. It was me making out with him so publicly.

She'd have done the same if Gavin had been a girl. I'd probably get yelled at later, but it was all worth it.

"We need to get your things," she said when we joined them.

"They're up in the cabin," I said. "The trunk's too big to carry it down the mountain."

This was it. This was goodbye.

I could feel tears gathering in my eyes. Gavin touched my cheek, and I nuzzled into his hand. "I'm sorry we have to leave."

"Me, too," he whispered. He kissed my forehead, and then my lips, and then pulled me into another hug. "We'll convince our parents to let us visit sometime. Maybe before school?"

We still had several weeks before my school started. That was a long time, but it was better than nothing. "Yeah. I hope you can convince your parents."

"I'll run away if it comes to that."

"You can live with us!" I said, not caring that my parents would probably vehemently disagree.

He laughed, knowing it was an empty promise. "I...I think I love you, Casey."

My breath caught. I never expected to hear those words together so soon, not even from Gavin. But, it was something I'd wanted to hear for so long. Those words, to that name, from someone other than my parents.

"I think I love you, too." The words hung between us, almost visible in their intensity, even though I only whispered mine. I'd never said them to anyone else before, not like this. But it felt right.

One last sweet kiss, and then he left.

I watched him go, and he looked back once, his hands thrust in his pockets, his shoulders hunched against the inevitable fight with his parents.

My heart ached for him. Already my skin cried out to be touched by him again. I only turned away when he'd finally gotten into the car, and they'd driven away up the mountain.

I returned to my parents and Ella. They were watching me as though they knew what had passed between us. Ella hugged me, understanding, and when we pulled apart she said, "I'll do whatever I can to help you two. You know that."

"I know that. Love you, Ella."

She smiled and said, "Love you, too, Casey." It was different with us, and I felt that difference now. She did love me, but not the way Gavin did, or even the way my parents did. But it was love, and I loved her back. My sister, my best friend.

By the time we were checked out and said all the other goodbyes—to Wade, to Alex, to Lily and Nick, and everyone else—Gavin was long gone from the cabin. My parents wanted a tour, so I gave them a quick one. And then all my stuff got loaded into the car, and it was time to go.

I hugged Ella one last time, promising to text her later, once my phone was charged up.

After one last look around the camp, I got into the car.

I looked toward cabin one, the forbidden cabin, but where so many memories had been made, both good and bad. I looked toward Lincoln Lodge, where Gavin first put his hand on my leg. Even to the latrines where I discovered Ryan on the verge of beating up my boyfriend.

My boyfriend.

My heart glowed at the word, and I felt a little dizzy with it. This was love, I told myself.

I got in the car but didn't belt in. As my dad drove us down the mountain, I twisted in my seat to gaze out the back window. So many memories. I'd thought it would be the first and only time I'd be able to come here, but now I knew I could come back. And I would.

I finally sat back properly as we passed the sign that read Ankley Springs.

Mom glanced back and saw that I was belted in. She smiled at me. "So tell me all about it!"

I did. I told her everything, all the way home.

The last thing I told her was how much I wanted to go back.

"We'll make sure of it," she confirmed.

My phone buzzed, and it was Gavin. I had just enough charge to check it. It was a snap of him—a selfie of him blowing a kiss at me. *Just wanted to tell you I love you again. See you soon.*

I took a quick picture of me doing the same, with the message: *Love you, too. I'm coming back, and so are you.*

I had to turn the phone off then, but I knew what his response would be. We would be together again. Soon.

About the Author

Gabriel D. Vidrine is a trans masculine scientist, dancer, and writer but is working towards reversing that order. They teach and perform belly dance all over the country, but still manage to cram in writing time whenever and wherever possible.

They are an avid reader and writer, and love science fiction, fantasy, horror, and paranormal romance, but will give any genre a try.

Gabriel lives with their husband, video game systems, and ridiculous cat, Selina, in Chicago, IL.

Email: vidrinegabriel@gmail.com

Facebook: www.facebook.com/GDVidrine

Twitter: @MxEmber

Website: www.vidrinegabriel.wixsite.com/fiction

Also Available from NineStar Press

Connect with NineStar Press

www.ninestarpress.com

www.facebook.com/ninestarpress

www.facebook.com/groups/NineStarNiche

www.twitter.com/ninestarpress

www.tumblr.com/blog/ninestarpress

www.ingramcontent.com/pod-product-compliance
Lightning Source LLC
Chambersburg PA
CBHW060558190726
48283CB00003B/1059